WALKING THE
CHOCTAW ROAD

Praise for Tim Tingle's *Walking the Choctaw Road*

For a good many years now, Tim Tingle has been one of my favorite American storytellers. Invariably, his narratives honor the Choctaw traditions of his ancestors. Yet they are told with such poetic clarity that any good listener, whether Indian or not, will feel invited into that world, a place of memory and song, courage, magical reality, and the extraordinary lives of everyday folks. Delivered in Tim's quiet, down-home Indian voice, they're the sort of lesson stories that stick to you like a burr.

The good news for readers is that these written versions of Tim's tales lose none of the gentle intensity of his memorable oral tellings. Their subjects range from the Trail of Tears to memories of his own childhood. They run the gamut from magical narratives of shape-shifters and escaping slaves seeking refuge among the Choctaws to an elder's recollections of finding friendship in the bitter barracks of an Indian boarding school. *Walking the Choctaw Road*, like one of those old Choctaw chants that kept the people's feet going along the long journey, will stay with you and lend you some of its strength. Cross the river with these stories—they'll give you safe passage. —Joseph Bruchac, author of *Tell Me a Tale*

———————————

A true talespinner celebrates his heritage with 11 absorbing yarns…Sophisticated narrative devices and some subtle character nuances give these stories a literary cast, but the author's evocative language, expert pacing, and absorbing subject matter will rivet readers and listeners both. —from *Booklist*

———————————

A superb storyteller…Poetic language and a compelling but quiet voice honor the Native American traditions for both the native and the non-native reader. —from *Kirkus Reviews*

———————————

Tingle is as skilled a storyteller as a collector. His compilation of Choctaw folklore is a pleasure to read, from introduction to final tale. This volume is a fine addition to any library's folklore, storytelling, multicultural history, or literature collection. —from VOYA (Voice of Youth Advocates)

———————————

Study Guides for
Walking the Choctaw Road
are available at
www.okreadsok.org and *www.cincopuntos.com*

WALKING
▼▼▼▼▼▼▼ T H E ▼▼▼▼▼▼▼
CHOCTAW ROAD

TIM TINGLE

Cinco Puntos Press
El Paso

"Archie's War" first appeared in *Storytelling Magazine* (March/April 2001). The story "Tony Byars" makes use of a paraphrase of four lines from T.S. Eliot's "The Wasteland." The traditional hymn "Farther Along" is used in "The Choctaw Way."

Printed in the United States

First Edition
10 9 8 7 6 5 4 3 2 1

Library of Congress Cataloging-in-Publication Data

Tingle, Tim.
  Walking the Choctaw road : stories from red people memory / by Choctaw storyteller Tim Tingle.—1st ed.
       p.   cm.
Summary: A collection of twelve stories of the Choctaw People, including traditional lore arising from beliefs and myths, historical tales passed down through generations, and personal stories of contemporary life.
  ISBN 0-938317-73-3
     1. Choctaw Indians—History—Anecdotes. 2. Choctaw Indians—Folklore. 3. Tales—Southern States. [1. Choctaw Indians—History—Anecdotes. 2. Choctaw Indians—Folklore. 3. Indians of North America—Folklore. 4. Folklore—Southern States.] I. Title.
  E99.C8T56 2003
  398.2'089'973—dc21
                                                                2003001069

Cover painting by Norma Howard, © 2001. Untitled.
Book and cover design by David Timmons, an exile from El Paso.

CONTENTS

▼ ▼ ▼ ▼ ▼ ▼ ▼ ▼ ▼ ▼ ▼ ▼ ▼ ▼ ▼

To Doc Moore, friend and mentor

ACKNOWLEDGMENTS

Many more people than I could possibly name have contributed to "Walking the Choctaw Road," but I would like to thank the following individuals for their long-standing support.

Dr. Geary Hobson, Phillip Morgan, Leroy Seale, Dr. Paula Conlon, Dr. Grayson Noley, and the late Dr. Michael Flanagan of the University of Oklahoma have given valuable feedback throughout the crafting of these stories. Tom Wheelus, Estella Long, Evangeline Wilson, Billy Bryant, and Dr. Lee Hester of the OK Choctaw Alliance have contributed important cultural information, as have Helen Harris, Judy Allen, Norma Howard, Jay MacAlvain, Ryan Mackey, Greg Howard, and Kenneth Tingle.

In the storytelling community, Joe Bruchac, Gayle Ross, Lynn Moroney, Karen Morgan, Hattie Gentry, Doc McConnell, Michael Cotter, Lee Pennington, Johnny Moses, Rosemary Davis, John Davis, Elizabeth Ellis, Nancy Kavanaugh, Linda Goodman, and Eve Myers of McDougal Littell have shown faith beyond reason.

I especially want to thank the late Tony Byars, Estelline Tubby, Charlie Jones, and Archie Mingo for their important educational gifts to all Choctaws.

My heartfelt thanks to Chief Greg Pyle, whose vision and leadership continue to make all Oklahoma Choctaws proud of where we have come from and excited about where we are going.

$\mathscr{I}$NTRODUCTION

▼ ▼ ▼ ▼ ▼ ▼ ▼ ▼ ▼ ▼ ▼ ▼ ▼ ▼ ▼

C*hata hapia hoke!*" It is a common phrase, an unoffi-
cial Choctaw tribal logo phrase. You see it on tee
shirts, bumper stickers, gimmee caps, and calen-
dars. It says, "We are proud to be Choctaw!"

The people who wear these caps and shirts are smiling.
If three words could ever sum up the approach to life
revealed by a collective Indian people's story, this phrase is
the summation of the Choctaw story. "*Chata hapia hoke!*"

As the Holocaust undoubtedly informs all Jewish writ-
ing—oral or printed—of the post-World War II era, the
Trail of Tears lingers deep in the memory bank of every
Choctaw. We have all heard the stories. In our minds and
dreams, we have walked the frozen ground carrying our
dead. We have gone mad picking at the smallpox scabs.
Crossing the river, we have drowned—but the story never
ends there.

Rather than a tale of excruciating loss and tragedy, the
story carries on to the present day and becomes one of tri-
umph and survival, for we contemporary Choctaws are
descendants of the survivors, as well as the deceased. At least
one of our ancestors lived through either the Trail or the
one hundred years of Mississippi exile.

Indeed, the Trail of Tears divides us as a people into those who stayed in Mississippi and those who left for Oklahoma. In the eyes of many, we are two people—the Mississippi Band of Choctaw Indians and the Choctaw Nation of Oklahoma. However, in the heroics of survival, in the celebration of our miracle of being, we are seeds of a common thistle.

The Choctaw story is a story of miracles.

To many Choctaws, these miracles are not only accepted, they are often expected, and sometimes offered as evidence that Choctaws are, to varying degrees, a chosen people. The high number of otherworldly occurrences in *Walking the Choctaw Road* is thus a reflection of the Choctaw belief system.

Throughout the body of Choctaw stories, whether they are traditional or contemporary, the quality of heart is of supreme importance. Truthfulness and generosity are valued far above bravery and even cunning. One other character trait shines through the collective Choctaw narrative, that of respect. Those who show respect for their elders and heed their teachings overcome powerful supernatural enemies. Conversely, those who don't, meet terrible fates through their callous lack of respect.

In considering which stories to include in *Walking the Choctaw Road,* a primary consideration was the question, "What is Choctaw?" I chose to include stories that, in my estimation, best reflect the history and beliefs of the Choctaws—members of the Oklahoma Choctaw Nation and the Mississippi Band of Choctaw Indians. Seen as a body, the narratives will give the reader a sense of what it is to be Choctaw, and why the Choctaws have operated so successfully in mainstream American society.

In collecting Choctaw stories, I have done so as an

The Choctaw family of Logan and Mrs. Baker, early 1900s, Indian Territory

independent endeavor, seeking out friends and relatives of friends. I have listened to stories told by total strangers in locations as diverse as the waiting room of the Choctaw Health Center in Talihina, Oklahoma, and the old tribal graveyard at the capitol grounds in Tuskahoma. I have been honored to enter the homes of older Choctaws who knew they were near death and who probably considered the interview as something of a summation of their life story.

Although—as a storyteller—I make my living by talking, I have one quality that gives me a distinct advantage when it comes to collecting stories from older people: I would much rather listen than talk. People who know me are laughing when they read this. But my older friends—Tony Byars, Estelline Tubby, Archie Mingo—have never heard me tell a story. I always enjoy their stories too much to interrupt them with one of my own.

If *Walking the Choctaw Road* achieves its purpose, it will act as a bridge between other cultures and that of the Choctaw Indian, allowing the non-Choctaw reader a glimpse into the worldview of a powerful group of modern Native Americans.

One major task in achieving this cultural bridge is to create a voice on the written page. Establishing a mood for the story and creating the effect that the reader is actually the listener is critical in communicating Native American stories. The wide variety of voices present in *Walking the Choctaw Road* can be attributed to a single factor—many Choctaws gave me stories, many voices flow through me.

This patchwork technique, of pulling elements of Choctaw culture from many sources and stitching them into a coherent single narrative, is used in almost every story in *Walking the Choctaw Road*. I think of the present volume, therefore, as an interior history of my people, an emotional and spiritual history, told from a single lens, from the eye of one who travels and gathers narrative threads.

My serious search for Choctaw stories began in 1992, when I became dissatisfied with the scarcity of recently collected material in the field. I had been telling Choctaw stories for several years, stories I had learned from family and friends and relatives. But I knew many more stories existed, and I was determined to find them.

From articles in the *Bishnik*, the monthly tribal newspaper of the Oklahoma Choctaw Nation, I knew that Charlie Jones was the most highly respected living tribal storyteller. His roots grow deep in Choctaw country; he spoke only Choctaw until he was nine years old. In addition to representing District One on the Choctaw Tribal council, Charlie Jones served as official historian of the Oklahoma

Choctaw Nation. I began conversing with Jones by telephone, and in May of 1992, I traveled to southeast Oklahoma to join Jones and a thousand other Choctaws on a 21-mile re-enactment of the Trail of Tears.

Even before the journey began, an event occurred— first startling and then miraculous—which I feel I must mention. Among the walkers that day were many older Choctaws, numbering in the hundreds. To assist these revered tribal members in making the walk, comfort stations had been set up every half mile or so along the route. In the early morning darkness before the walk, vandals destroyed the comfort stations, pushing them over on their doors and rendering them unusable.

To most of us, this was a nuisance, as well as an insulting reminder that not everyone respected our time of honoring our ancestors. To the older Choctaws, something else seemed to be occurring. This one act brought back memories of fearful times of racial prejudice. But Choctaws know that no matter how dark and troubled times may appear to be, a miracle is always waiting to happen. As is so often the case, the miracle came in the form of good-hearted people willing to work.

Members of churches that lined our route had apparently heard of our dilemma, and they responded in an unforgettable act of generosity and good will. They opened their doors to those needing respite from the hot August day, and, entering their kitchens, they went to work!

Young children made peanut butter and tuna salad sandwiches while men and women fried chicken and made potato salad. They offered pies, cookies, baked beans, and fresh fruit to the walkers. Five-gallon jugs of iced tea and chairs and tables were set out on the church lawns. It seemed that every corner we turned, we were greeted with

Lola Ross, a young Choctaw woman, Indian territory, circa 1910

smiling faces, good food, and chairs to rest our weary feet.

I remember, at about the 15-mile mark, crossing a shallow roadside ditch and stepping onto a soft carpet of St. Augustine grass in front of a church. I eased myself down and leaned against the trunk of a sycamore tree. I was too tired to wander over to the table of food, even though I had spotted a pan of cornbread and a gallon jar of whole dill pickles, both high on my list of food favorites.

Not two minutes went by when I spotted a little girl of about five coming my way. Her tiny fingers clung desperately to a glass of iced tea and a plate loaded with food. She saw me looking at her and gave me a big smile—then held her breath as she hurried the last 20 feet, making sure I appreciated her heroic effort.

I thanked her for the iced tea and downed most of it before setting the glass aside.

"My mother made it," she said, looking at the cornbread on the paper plate. So, I took a big bite and told her how good it was. It was better than good. It was moist with butter and so crunchy and soft it crumbled in my palms. Just before she ran away, my new friend said, "People shouldn't be mean."

I knew she had overheard her mother say it, maybe earlier that morning as her mother explained to the family where she would be spending her Saturday. More than any single phrase that entire weekend—a weekend filled with powerful stories and speeches of heroism—I remember that phrase. I was sitting in the grass, leaning against a tree, sweaty and tired and mumbling my thanks with food in my mouth, food cooked by total strangers and given freely, and a little girl said to me, "People shouldn't be mean."

She was only five years old, but she got it. She understood. She had already turned and run away, so she probably didn't hear me say, "Most of the time they're not, sweetheart. Most of the time they're not."

Walking the Choctaw Road is filled with stories of people who, like those good church folks, reached across boundaries to offer a hand to those in need. I like to think it is the Choctaw way of doing things.

Leaving the church grounds, refreshed and filled, I sought out Charlie Jones. I found him walking by himself and approached him cautiously, telling him who I was and letting him take the lead in the conversation. He soon began telling stories.

I was impressed by the detailed descriptions that characterized Jones' stories, and encouraged by the importance he attributed to the oral narrative. This was also my first encounter with a style of performing that is employed by the vast majority of Choctaw storytellers I have met. Even though Jones told his stories as we walked, he appeared to withdraw from our surroundings, a two-lane highway in rural southeast Oklahoma shared by a thousand other Choctaw walkers. His voice deepened, lowered in volume, and took on a slight rhythmic quality.

This semi-trance state, I have since noted, encourages listeners also to tune out their surroundings. Both the performer and the audience appear to experience the narrative rather than observe it from a distant perspective. Following each story, Jones observed a period of silence, sometimes lasting as long as 20 minutes. The length of time appeared to be related to the level of seriousness of the story; a lighter tale would soon be followed by soft laughter and conversation, while a tragedy seemed to require a respectful and lengthy silence.

During my initial visit with Charlie Jones, I took no

notes, but instead created a detailed written account of our meeting upon my return to Texas the following day. In September of that same year I traveled to Mississippi to the Choctaw Pearl River Reservation, where I met Estelline Tubby.

Estelline Tubby is considered by her community of Pearl River Reservation, Philadelphia, Mississippi, to be the foremost Choctaw storyteller living. She has, since our initial meeting in September of 1993, become my most important entry into the unique world of the Mississippi Choctaw. The occasion of our first meeting is, in retrospect, a tale of subtle backwoods diplomacy, a story of an outsider (myself), who is totally ignorant of the cultural guideposts, somehow stumbling and stepping in the right direction.

In the fall of 1993, I planned my first trip to central Mississippi, hoping to visit Naniay Wayah and other tribal sites. When I asked the Mississippi Arts Council for possible names of Choctaw storytellers and traditional musicians, I was given the names of Tubby and Archie Mingo, respectively. Locating them on the reservation was another matter entirely.

At the Choctaw Tribal Museum, I introduced myself to Dr. Robert Fergusen, a former professor at Vanderbilt University, who at that time served as tribal historian. Married to a local Choctaw, Martha, Fergusen also operated a small recording and video studio out of the museum offices. After a brief tour of the museum, during which we were joined by several other visitors, I asked Martha Fergusen if she knew how I might get in touch with Estelline Tubby. She hesitated before replying, "I'm not sure. I'll see what I can do. Will you be here tomorrow?" Several return trips to the museum on subsequent days yielded only similar enigmatic responses.

Late one afternoon after the museum had emptied, I dashed inside to make a purchase. Martha Fergusen was alone and seemed glad to see me. She locked the doors and led me to a back office before saying, "Estelline Tubby lives only a few blocks away. She knows you are looking for her. She knew several weeks ago."

I remember thinking that several weeks ago would be even before I had made the commitment to come to Mississippi.

"If you want to hear her stories, here is what you do. Go to her home this afternoon. She won't let you in. You probably won't even see her. But she will see you. Tell her what you want and that you will come back tomorrow for her answer. She wants to see you and have a chance to dream about you. If she has an owl dream, you will never see her. Good luck!"

I waited for a few hours and then followed her directions to Tubby's modest brick home less than half a mile from the museum. As I approached the door, I knew I was being watched. In fact, as I drove down the street, all the eyes of the neighborhood appeared to be marking my path.

Tubby answered the door after a light knock, though I could not see her through the screen door. We had the briefest of conversations and she told me to return the next day, a Sunday, at two p.m., and she would let me know if I could hear her stories.

When I returned the next day at the appointed time, Estelline Tubby greeted me warmly at the door wearing a traditional blue and white dress, one I later found out she had made. She is a slight woman, but nothing about her is frail. In fact, she appears unaware of the aura of strength she projects.

She ushered me to her living room and asked me what

Governor Thompson McKinney of the Choctaw Nation, 1886–1887

I wanted to know. I shrugged my shoulders and smiled, feeling very happy to be there, and soon Tubby began to talk. Following a few introductory statements, her eyelids dropped, her voice took on a trance quality, and she began a barely visible rocking motion. She then closed her eyes and spoke as if she were witnessing the story.

I was at first disconcerted by the level of Tubby's transformation during her storytelling performance. She began by telling of the old prophecies that predicted the removal of the Choctaws from their homeland and carried through to her earliest memories of her grandmother, who had been a medicine woman.

Following my first meeting with Tubby, I began to realize the potential importance of the stories I was being given. I had previously been unable to locate any narratives documenting the time period of Tubby's stories.

During that same visit to Philadelphia, I also met Archie Mingo, a celebrated Choctaw chant singer. He became a valued friend and mentor, teaching me several vocable songs and enlightening me as to the Choctaw technique of gate-keeping, or protecting community members from unwanted visitors. As a mixed-blood member of the Oklahoma Choctaw Nation, I am an outsider to many Mississippi Choctaws. I will always be indebted to Mingo and Tubby for their demonstrated trust in sharing their songs and stories with me.

Shortly after my return to Texas, I began to make Choctaw friends in the Austin and San Antonio area, and eventually met Tony Byars. Although our time together was short, stretching over a two-year period, Byars had a profound impact on the direction of my collecting. He imparted the idea that I now had a responsibility in regard to the stories, that nothing had been accidental about my collecting these seemingly disconnected narratives. Byars encouraged me to present Choctaw stories in schools and at festivals, like the Texas Folklife Festival in San Antonio.

By 1996, storytelling had become my primary means of livelihood. Less than a year after the death of Tony Byars in 1997, I moved to Oklahoma to be closer to the source of Oklahoma Choctaw stories. Through a series of fortuitous encounters, I have broadened my circle of informants from

Choctaw Willie Billy, Indian Territory, circa 1910

a handful of storytellers to a network of dozens of friends always eager to hear and share stories.

I have arranged the stories in this collection in chronological order to enable the reader to witness the changes that time and history have rendered upon Choctaw beliefs. The various narratives cover a time span of almost two centuries of tribal life. I chose to illustrate the stories with photos selected from historical archives to present visually the idea promoted by the text—that we Choctaws are a rich and diverse people, culturally American and spiritually Choctaw.

The collection and sharing of Choctaw stories is, as I have said, a life work, an ongoing and never-ending process, for people live and die and stories unfold continuously. I hope *Walking the Choctaw Road* will inspire you, the reader, to recognize the valuable treasures surrounding you. The stories of your family and friends are your key to who you are and how you came to be.

CROSSING
BOK CHITTO

▼ ▼ ▼ ▼ ▼ ▼ ▼ ▼ ▼ ▼ ▼ ▼ ▼ ▼ ▼

Mississippi, 1800

As European nations battled for supremacy in the New World, powerful alliances were formed with Native American nations. The recently freed Thirteen Colonies found an ally in the Mississippi Choctaws, who played a key role in enabling Andrew Jackson to defeat the British at the Battle of New Orleans. Following the War of 1812, cotton plantations grew and white settlers looked to expand their land holdings. Pearl River Reservation Mississippi Choctaws still tell passed-down family stories of helping runaway slaves seeking refuge.

THERE IS A RIVER called Bok Chitto that cuts through Mississippi. In the days before the War Between the States, in the days before the Trail of Tears, Bok Chitto was a boundary. On one side of the river lived the Choctaws, a sovereign nation of people. On the other side lived the plantation owners and their slaves. If a slave escaped and made his way across Bok Chitto, the slave was free; the slave owner could not follow. That was the law.

So, long ago and far away, when Bok Chitto was the

Indian log cabin homestead, Indian Territory, circa 1900

boundary, a Choctaw momma woke her little daughter up one Sunday morning.

"Martha Tom, you lazy little girl! You get yourself out of bed. Get up and put your dress on. The sun has been up for two hours and I have a wedding to cook for today. Take this basket, fill it with blackberries and hurry back."

Dragging herself out of bed, Martha Tom went looking for blackberries. When she couldn't find any on the Choctaw side of the river, she did something she'd been told never to do. She went crossing Bok Chitto to the other side—for the only way to cross Bok Chitto in those days was a stone path just beneath the surface of the river. Only the Choctaws knew it was there, for the Choctaws had built it. When the river flooded, they built the stones up. When the river sank in times of drought, they built the stones down, always just beneath the muddy surface of the water.

Martha Tom went crossing Bok Chitto. She went deep into those Mississippi woods, deeper than any woods we've ever seen, for there are no woods today like those old

Mississippi woods. She found the blackberries and filled her basket, but when she looked to the sky for the sun to lead her home—it was cloudy and she was lost. She thought she heard a voice and followed it, going still deeper into those woods.

She found a clearing headed by a stump, covered with grape vines. The clearing was filled with logs, rolled out as if they were benches. Then she heard someone coming and dove into the vines. Through the leaves she saw a skinny little black man with a bushy head of white hair, hobbling with a cane. He put the cane aside and very carefully stepped onto the stump. While Martha Tom watched, he lifted his heels and began to stomp, then wave his arms, then talk.

"He is crazy," thought Martha Tom. "There is nobody there!"

Then the man called out, "We are bound for the promised land!"

What happened next would change Martha Tom's life forever. For a hundred voices came in reply, unseen voices, like spirit voices shivering the low hanging moss in the trees, whispering, "We are bound for the promised land!"

This seemed to invigorate the old man and he went to stomping and calling again, "We are bound for the promised land!"

Once again the voices came in reply, human voices this time, closer and closer they came, calling, "We are bound for the promised land!" The old man bowed his head and said, "Oh, who will come and go with me?"

A hundred slaves replied, stepping from behind the trees and rising up from the bushes where they were hiding.

"We will come and go with you.
We are bound for the promised Land!"

It was the calling together of the forbidden slave church,

deep in those Mississippi woods. The man began to preach and the people began to sing. Martha Tom had never heard music like this before, but it touched her deeply. Then something else touched her, on the shoulder. She looked up to see the biggest man she had ever seen, his chest so big it was about to pop the buttons off his shirt!

"You're lost, little girl?" he said in a deep voice that seemed to smile.

Martha Tom nodded.

"You're Choctaw, from across Bok Chitto?"

She nodded again.

"You're afraid and want to go home?"

Once more she nodded.

"What is your name, little girl?"

"Martha Tom."

"Well, Martha Tom, I'll get my son to take you back to the river. You can find your way home from there. Little Mo!" he called.

There appeared a boy of about ten. "Little Mo, this girl is lost. She is Choctaw from across Bok Chitto. Take her to the riverbank and she can get home from there."

Little Mo looked at his daddy. He looked at Martha Tom and said, "Daddy, I can't do it."

"I'm your father and I am telling you. What do you mean you can't do it?"

"Daddy, the men from the plantation house told us if the children are seen playing near the river, our whole family will get in trouble. I can't do it."

But his father seemed undaunted. He knelt down to the boy and said, "Son, son, it's about time you learned. There is a way to move amongst them where they won't even notice you. It's like you're invisible. You move not too fast, not too slow, eyes to the ground, away you go! Now give it a try and get this little girl home!"

Well, it sounded like a fun game to play, so Little Mo took Martha Tom by the hand and off they went, just as Little Mo's daddy had taught him, not too fast, not too slow, eyes to the ground, away you go!

They skirted the plantation house and walked right in front of the porch, where the owners were doing their sipping and sighing that Sunday morning. But no one paid them any mind. "We must be invisible," thought Little Mo.

Soon they were at the river and it was Martha Tom's turn to lead. She took him to the stone path, but he couldn't see it beneath the surface of the water.

"This will be a fun game to play," she thought. She took five paces back to get a good running start, then leapt into the river! Little Mo reached out to grab her dress as she flew by, to keep her from drowning. But when she landed in the river, she stood up!

"Little girl, what kind of witch are you?" Little Mo cried.

Martha Tom laughed, "I'm not any kind of witch. You can do it, too! Come on!" She took Little Mo by the hand and together the two of them went crossing Bok Chitto to the Choctaw side.

Even before they stepped from the stones to the earth, Little Mo heard it, the sound of the drums. At first he thought it must be the heartbeat of the earth itself. It was the old men calling the Choctaws to the wedding ceremony.

As he and Martha Tom looked down the street of log homes, they saw women step out of every doorway, Choctaw women dressed in long white cotton dresses skimming the ground. Their shiny black hair fell well below their waists.

The women formed a line and began a procession to the clearing at the end of town. They began a stomp dance

Louisiana Choctaws in full wedding attire, Bayou Lacomb, Lousiana, 1908

to the beat of the drums, but it was far less a stomp and far more the lift and glide of a dance. When they reached the clearing, they formed two circles, the women and the men, and the wedding ceremony began.

The old men began to sing the wedding song. It is still sung today in Mississippi and Oklahoma, just as they sang it then.

"Way, hey ya hey ya
You a hey you ay
A hey ya a hey ya!

"Way, hey ya hey ya
You a hey you ay
A hey ya a hey ya!

"You a hey you ay
A hey ya hey ya
You a hey you ay
A hey ya hey ya
You a hey you a
A hey ya a hey yo!"

Little Mo had never heard music like this before, but it touched him deeply. Then something else touched them both, on the shoulder. It was Martha Tom's mother!

"Little girl, little girl, you are in for it now. You have been crossing Bok Chitto! Now I'm not mad at him, but you take him to the river and come right back. And give me those blackberries! You are in for it now!"

Martha Tom knew better than to smile, but she wasn't afraid. She knew her mother could cackle like a mad crow on the outside, while inside she would coo like a dove with love for her daughter. Martha Tom took Little Mo to the river and showed him how to cross on his own. And this began a friendship that would last for years.

Every Sunday morning Martha Tom would cross Bok Chitto on her way to church. She sat with Little Mo's family now. She listened to the preaching and she sang the songs in English. Then every evening she would sing them in Choctaw as she went crossing Bok Chitto on her way home.

Then one day trouble came. It always does, in stories or in life, trouble comes. There was a slave sale and 20 slaves were sold. They were to leave for New Orleans the very next day before sunrise. The men from the households were called together to listen to the names being read. Little Mo's mother was on that list.

As her husband walked home, he wondered how to tell

his family what had happened. He decided to let them have their last meal in peace.

When the children stood to clear the table, he motioned for them to be seated. Feeling his knees grow weak, he supported himself with his right palm on the table while his left hand stroked his wife on the neck and shoulders.

"Your mother has been sold," he said.

"Nooo!" she cried. The tears seemed to squirt down her cheeks. The children looked at their parents and began to cry. They had never seen their mother and father like this.

"This is our last evening together!" he shouted. "Stop your crying. I want every one of you to find something small and precious, something to give your mother to remember you by, something she can hide, something they can't take away. Now, get up and help your mother pack. You will not see her again."

No one moved.

"I am your father! Get up and help your mother pack!"

No one moved. Then Little Mo pulled his father's sleeve and said, "Daddy, there is a way we can stay together."

"No, son. It is a slave sale. It is final."

"Daddy, we can go crossing Bok Chitto."

"Son, they'll have the dogs guarding the river tonight, to prevent a crossing."

"Daddy, listen to me. We can go just like you taught me, not too fast, not too slow, eyes to the ground, away you go! We'll be invisible. Daddy, we have to give it a try."

For the first time that day, hope filled his father's heart. "You are right, son. We have to give it a try."

He grabbed seven burlap bags and gave one to each member of his family, saying, "Pack quick, pack light, pack for running. We may have to."

They did pack quick, they packed light, but not quick enough, for the men in the plantation house saw them working late. They called out those with the dogs and the lanterns and the guns, and they surrounded that little house in the woods.

When Little Mo's daddy stood with his family around him, he looked out the back door and said, "We could go out that way. It would be dark and maybe safer. But this night's journey is not about darkness and safety. It is about faith. It is about freedom. We will go out the front door."

And so they did, out the front door, down the front steps, out the front gate—walking just as Little Mo had reminded them, not too fast, not too slow, eyes to the ground, away you go!

Then something remarkable happened. This family became invisible!

They walked right into the circle of lanterns, so close the light should have shone on their clothes, but the light shone right through them. They walked so close to the dogs they could have reached out and stroked the dogs' fur, but the dogs did not know they were there.

Soon they stood on the banks of Bok Chitto. Little Mo looked to the clouds covering the moon and said, "Daddy, I can't get us across. I've never been here at night. I can't do it!"

But his father was undaunted. He picked Little Mo up and sat him on his hip till their faces almost touched.

"Son, the time has come. You know what we call you— Little Mo. But you know also that is not your name. Son, son, the hour is at hand! Your name is Moses. Now, Moses, get us across that water!"

Moses leapt down from his father's hip and went running to the river. He dipped his arms deep into the chilly waters and went back and forth till he found the path. Then quick as a bird he flew across the stones and burst into Martha Tom's home.

"I'm sorry, I know it's late. But we are trying to come

across. The men are after us, the men with the dogs and the lanterns and the guns. Can you help us?"

Martha Tom's mother, as you know, was the take-charge type. She jumped out of bed and talked as she dressed.

"Son, you run right back to your family and hide them in the bushes near the path. Go, now, run! You'll know when to come across. Go! I have work to do!"

She went to every home in that village, pushed open the doors and called inside, "Women! Put on your white dresses! Bring a candle and meet me at the river. We're going to have a ceremony tonight, the crossing kind!"

And so it came to pass. Those men on the far side of the river, those men with the dogs and the lanterns and the guns, they saw emerging from the dark fog on the Choctaw side what looked to them like a band of angels, angels carrying candles and casting a halo glow in the fog around their faces.

Then, rising from the bushes and coming to life in front of them, they saw seven runaway slaves. They lifted their guns to fire. Then they froze, for stepping out of that band of angels they saw the most beautiful little angel of them all. Her right hand held a candle, her left hand was outstretched, and she was floating on the water!

She was singing as she moved, a song they had heard the slaves sing many times, but never in the tongue she sang it.

> *"Nitak ishtayo pikmano*
> *Chissus ut minitit.*
> *Umala holitopama*
> *Chihot aya lashke!*

> "We are bound for the Promised Land,
> We are bound for the Promised Land!

O, who will come and go with me?
We are bound for the Promised land."

She took Little Mo by the hand, he took his mother, she took her husband, and together all seven of them went crossing Bok Chitto. When they reached the fog on the far side of the river, they blew the candles out and disappeared into the darkness, never to be seen on the slave side again.

But the descendants of those people, they still talk about that night. The Choctaws talk about the cunning of that little girl. The black people talk about the faith of that little boy. But maybe the Anglos tell it best. For they talk about the night their forefathers witnessed seven black spirits, walking on the water—to their freedom!

THE BEATING
OF WINGS

▼ ▼ ▼ ▼ ▼ ▼ ▼ ▼ ▼ ▼ ▼ ▼ ▼ ▼ ▼

Mississippi, 1820

Contemporary Choctaws are a predominately Christian people, but stories of shape-shifting witches and owls still thrive among Choctaws, whether they live in Texas, Mississippi, Oklahoma, or Alabama. The owl is also considered to be the messenger of death.

JIMMY BEN LAY ON HIS BACK looking at the full round moon through his window. It was three in the morning, the same hour of his awakening for over a month. Something was coming for him and he knew it.

Jimmy lay quiet as a stone, just as he had every morning for the past several weeks. Cold beads of sweat trickled down his forehead. He breathed slowly, deliberately. He sensed the presence of everything that passed near or through his window—the charred aroma of the evening's cooking fire, the squall of a panther, the beating of wings, even the heavy odor of a water moccasin sliding through the mud at the yard's edge.

Something was coming, something he must hunt or kill or face. In a flash of certainty, he knew what it was. He wondered how he could have gone a month without knowing.

"The beating of wings," he said aloud. "It will come with the beating of wings."

Jimmy took one long deep breath and on the soft purr of his exhale, it came. When he heard it land on his windowsill, he had to force himself to look. It was a snow owl. As Jimmy Ben watched, the owl gripped the windowsill with his claws and slowly opened his cotton-white wings. His wingspan was wider than Jimmy was tall, and he wanted the boy to know it.

Relaxing his wings, the bird lifted a leg and dug his claw deep into the side of the window frame. As Jimmy watched, the owl scraped a long scar into the wood, marking it. Then he turned, cast a powerful scream into the night and flew away. Jimmy's heart pounded like a wounded rabbit's. His breath came in hard short gasps.

He leapt out the window and followed the owl through the pinewoods. The owl flew from one low limb to the next, then lifted high over the treetops before settling in a clearing. Jimmy was close behind, stepping over fallen logs and brushing low-hanging moss aside with his arms, moving as quickly as he dared in the darkness. When he arrived at the clearing, he crouched down, hiding in a clump of honeysuckle vines.

The owl was sitting on a stump, gently lifting and lowering his wings. As Jimmy Ben watched with eyes as big as the moon, the owl flapped his wings and hovered three feet above the tree stump. He seemed to float there for several minutes, then he stepped on the stump with the legs of a man.

It was the body of an owl and the legs of a man.

Jimmy froze, too scared to breathe. The owl gazed slowly

around the clearing, peering deep in the woods with his night-seeing eyes. Then he began to flap his wings again. Jimmy knew he wasn't going anywhere, not with the weight of a man's legs to carry.

The owl flapped his wings faster and faster till the feathers started flying. He beat the air with his wings like he was striking out at somebody.

Whoosh! Whoosh!

Over and over he whipped his wings till all his feathers were floating in the air or lying on the ground. Jimmy saw white skin stretched across the wing bones of the owl. From under the skin, tiny fingers pushed and poked, then popped right through. Human arms stretched out, cracking and breaking the bones of the owl.

It was the body of a man and the head of an owl.

Jimmy wanted to run, but knew he would be killed if he did. He watched as the owl-man covered his head with his arms, then lifted his face. It was the face of a man with the eyes of an owl.

Jimmy Ben knew this man. It was Tom Bigbee. "Stay away from Tom Bigbee," his daddy once told him. "His medicine is bad."

Tom Bigbee looked to Jimmy's hiding place and stepped clumsily from the stump in that direction. He had just regained his balance from the steep step-down when the first light of day cast a yellow glow on the clearing. Shaking his head and moaning, Tom Bigbee lifted an arm to shield his eyes and fled into the darkness of the swamp.

He had a way of walking like nobody else Jimmy Ben had ever seen. "With all that changing, he's gone and left part of himself somewhere else," he remembered his daddy saying. He didn't understand it at the time. Now he did. Tom's left leg seemed frozen at the knee joint, and his foot was twisted and dragged behind him like a yard broom when he walked.

The old man used his bad leg like a crutch. Leaning all his weight on it, he would stretch and stomp out with the good leg and drag the other one behind him.

Jimmy Ben waited till the man was gone, then dashed home, hoping his mother hadn't noticed he was gone. Barely two minutes after he climbed into bed, she stuck her head through the door.

"Get on up, son. Those weeds are growing while you sleep." He knew he was in for another long day of chopping corn.

Jimmy Ben told nobody what happened that morning, nor did he mention it at supper.

That night he had a terrible dream. He dreamed he followed that owl through the woods, and when they came to the clearing, the owl walked around the stump where Jimmy Ben couldn't see. The owl was pecking and clawing at something lying on the ground.

When Jimmy crept out from his hiding place to get a better look, he saw himself lying there. The owl was pecking out his eyes. Jimmy Ben screamed and the owl looked up. The face of Tom Bigbee glared at him and said, "You been following me?"

The next thing he knew, Tom Bigbee was on him, clawing at his face. He waved his arms and cried out, "No! Go away!" Tom Bigbee grabbed his arms by the wrists and forced them to his side.

"Wake up, Jimmy. You are having a nightmare!" He opened his eyes and saw his father. "You are almost as strong as a man, son," he said. "You've been fighting me. Come on now. You can sleep in our room." Jimmy spent the remainder of the night on a pallet by his parent's bed.

The next morning his mother took him to see Miss Tubby, a healing lady who lived on the edge of the swamp in a grove of cypress trees. Miss Tubby took Jimmy Ben to her backyard, gave him a cane basket and said, "You got your knife with you?" When he nodded, she said, "Follow me."

Miss Tubby was a fast walker and Jimmy had to hurry to keep up. Once they passed a rattlesnake sunning on a rock. Jimmy slowed down to a whispering walk, but Miss Tubby kept right on. "She didn't see it," thought Jimmy.

"It wasn't going to bother us," Miss Tubby said.

After an hour of walking, they came to a narrow strip of land on the banks of a clear water creek. A dozen cedar trees covered the tiny peninsula, most of them of recent growth, but one large tree grew parallel to the ground. The base of the tree was scorched and scarred from an ancient battle with ball lightning.

"Struck on the east side," Miss Tubby said. "The woods for miles around burned, but this old tree survived. It may be bent but it's still living."

Miss Tubby climbed over the tree. "Give me your knife," she said. She cut and sliced several lengths of bark till the basket was filled. Then she produced a small cup from her apron pocket and dipped it in the creek.

"Good clean water," she said, sipping slowly and handing Jimmy Ben the cup. He knelt to the creek to fill it, then saw she was already walking, faster than before. He splashed one cup on his face and gulped down another as he ran to catch Miss Tubby.

As they neared her house, she turned to him and said, "Your mother and I are going to visit on the porch. There's a fire hole in the backyard, not too far from the well. You'll find kindling by the barn. Let me know when the fire is burning low and steady."

Thirty minutes later Jimmy walked around the house to find his mother slowly rocking, fanning herself with a feather fan. Miss Tubby sat with her head back and her mouth open, napping and snoring like his daddy's hunting dog.

"Should I wake her up?" he asked his mother.

"Don't be worrying about me," said Miss Tubby. "You ought to be worrying about leaving that fire."

"Yes ma'm," said Jimmy. He dashed to the fire and she rose to follow.

She tied the cedar strips to one end of a green pine branch and held it over the fire. When it was smoking, she circled Jimmy Ben, waving the smoke all around him, singing as she walked.

"Lift your arms up over your head," she told him. She smoked Jimmy and sang for half an hour, then motioned for him to join her on the back porch steps.

"That owl will come back for you," she said. "I have done everything I can do. You are strong. You must help yourself now. Keep working to the good and have faith that good will come of it."

She stood up and, resting one hand on her thigh, helped herself up the steps and into the house. "Tell your mother I said good-bye," she said over her shoulder. For the first time that day, Jimmy saw that she was tired.

"I may be tired, Jimmy Ben, but I can still outrun you," Miss Tubby said on the way to her bedroom.

For the next three nights, Jimmy slept on the floor in his parents' room. When nothing out of the ordinary happened, he returned to his own bed. Every morning for a week, his mother asked about him.

"Did you sleep well?"

"Ummm," he would nod, and roll over for another hour of sleep before his father came for him.

Jimmy Ben now slept better than before. He no longer woke up at three in the morning and if he dreamed at all, he couldn't remember. Weeks went by and Jimmy only thought about the owl a few times a day, usually at nightfall when the screech owls made their presence known.

One morning, his grandfather stopped by for breakfast. While Jimmy cleared the dishes, he heard his grandfather say, "Somebody was telling me Tom Bigbee was fishing for a few weeks down on the coast. They say he is back now. I 'spec maybe he's still keeping to himself in the woods, far as anybody knows. I been talking to Miss Tubby 'bout it."

Jimmy's mother and father didn't say anything, but he saw them glance a quick look at each other. His father sipped his coffee and his mother stared into her cup.

"I brought something for Jimmy," his grandfather said. He walked to his horse and returned with a blowdart gun. "Mind if I borrow him today? I'd like to show him how I used to hunt when I was a boy."

"I hunt squirrels with my blowdart," said Jimmy Ben.

"Purty good, sounds like," said his grandfather. "Maybe we go looking for rabbit today."

"That'll be fine," said Jimmy's father. "Maybe you can stay over tonight, if you like. We'll put an extra rabbit in the stew."

"We'll catch that extra rabbit," said Jimmy Ben's grandfather, smiling as he said it. "Jimmy, these old legs don't go so fast no more. How 'bout we take the horse?"

Jimmy Ben climbed on behind his grandfather and they rode north for an hour, to the woods below a group of low-lying hills. His grandfather dismounted, helped him off the

Toshkachito, a Choctaw hunter, demonstrating an unusually long blowgun,
St. Tammany Parish, Louisiana, 1908

horse, and said, "Let's sit and talk for a spell, Jimmy. I want to tell you 'bout a different kind of hunting." He removed a handful of feathered darts from his saddlebag. One end of each was tipped with a sharp thorn.

"Your blow gun can protect you, Jimmy, if you learn to use it. A man-owl is after you. That's serious business. Don't think he's not coming back. He is. He never will leave you alone, not as long as he is alive."

"What can I do?"

"First off, do what Miss Tubby said. Keep working for the good. But that's not always enough. When Tom Bigbee comes, you got to be ready. Now let's see if we can find us a rabbit."

Jimmy Ben followed his grandfather into a clump of golden sycamore trees. They had only walked a short distance when his grandfather held up his hand and pointed to a thick cedar bush. He reached for the gun and Jimmy gave it to him. The old man loaded the gun and shifted into a crouch, moving without a sound.

Jimmy Ben thought he saw movement in the bush, but he couldn't be sure. Then his grandfather drew in his breath and fired the dart, several feet to the left of the bush. At the same moment, a rabbit leapt from the bush. He caught the dart in his neck, twisted in mid-air, and fell to the ground.

"I didn't see the rabbit," Jimmy said.

"I didn't either," said his grandfather. "That's the other part of what Miss Tubby told you. Go with your faith."

Jimmy Ben and his grandfather spent the rest of the day moving quietly through the woods. Twice Jimmy halted and fired at movement in the undergrowth, but nothing came of it.

"That's alright, grandson. It will be there when you need it," said his grandfather.

The next morning, Jimmy's grandfather woke him. The boy lay on his back in bed with his eyes closed. His grandfather placed his hand on Jimmy's forehead and prayed in Choctaw for a long time.

Jimmy's eyes were still closed when his grandfather saddled his horse and rode away. He knew, as did his grandfather, that the owl would come that night.

By his parent's actions that day, Jimmy guessed that his grandfather had not alerted them to the owl's coming. This was something for Jimmy Ben to face alone.

The day passed in a crawl as he tried to sweat out his fear, working with his hoe in the cornfield. He ate much slower than usual at supper. He felt like a distant witness to everything around him. After supper, he gathered dried husks from the corncrib and spread them beneath his window and in the yard on his side of the house, as a noisy warning to himself.

Jimmy went to bed early, his gun lying beside him on the floor. It was loaded with a dart his grandfather had dipped in the strongest poison he knew. He lay wide awake for hours, but finally became so wrapped up in his imaginings of sneaking, owl-eyed Tom Bigbee that he drifted over into the world of dreams.

The real Tom Bigbee woke him out of it. Jimmy's eyes popped open. He heard heavy breathing, then a stomping sound followed by a long dragging noise. Tom Bigbee was approaching the house.

Through his window he saw a full moon hanging in a cloudless sky, a bright yellow and blue vision on the wall of his bedroom. The sound came closer. A dry rustling noise floated through the window as Tom Bigbee dragged his bad leg through the cornhusks. Then the moon disappeared and the scraggly, bearded face of Tom Bigbee rested on the windowsill.

Jimmy Ben reached for his gun and quick owl eyes followed the movement. Tom's face vanished. Thinking Tom Bigbee may be crouched beneath his window, Jimmy scooted backwards, bracing himself against the far wall. He lifted his gun to his mouth and took in short breaths, ready to fire at any moment.

Several minutes passed. Jimmy took a small step and moved to the window to get a better view. For a brief moment he saw the yellow of the moon. A shadow flashed before it. Then Jimmy Ben heard the beating of wings.

He saw a small white ball flying at him, then giant wings spread across the moon and Jimmy's room was cast in darkness. The owl drew in his wings and the room was filled again with light. The owl flew directly in front of the moon and with every beat of his wings the room fluttered from light to darkness. With his sharp claws aimed at the eyes of the boy, the owl threw back his wings and sped into his dive. The window to the boy's room was just before him.

Jimmy Ben was blinded by the flickering of darkness into light. He tried shading his eyes. He knew the owl was almost upon him. He could see nothing, but he could feel the wind from the owl's wings on his face. The time had come. He closed his eyes, drew in a breath, and fired. The dart whistled through the air and the owl flew to meet it. A scream, half-owl and half-man, tore through the fabric of the yellow and blue night. The beating of wings ceased.

Jimmy Ben ran to the window. Though everything appeared as a vague outline of shapes and shadows, he thought he saw the owl flapping his wings and rolling on the ground. The owl seemed to grow to the size of a small child and drag itself into the woods. As his vision cleared, he saw bloodstained white feathers strewn among the corn-husks on the ground below his window.

Jimmy Ben sat on the edge of his bed till he saw the first red streak of dawn through the pine trees. He placed his blowdart gun against the window frame and went to wake his parents.

"The owl is dead," he said, leaning his head through the doorway.

"What?" said his father.

"I shot the owl. He is dead. Will you go with me to the clearing?"

Half an hour later Jimmy led his father through the woods, following the same trail he had taken in pursuit of the owl a month earlier. Stepping into the clearing, he was amazed at how small everything seemed. The stump was barely two feet tall. As he and his father stood watching, the bright rays of dawn washed the entire woods in a clean white light.

Even Tom Bigbee looked peaceful. He was lying dead at

the base of the stump, a blowdart in his neck. White feathers clung to the skin around the wound.

Jimmy Ben and his family continued working to the good. Neither Tom Bigbee nor any other witch owl ever bothered them again.

TRAIL OF
TEARS

▼ ▼ ▼ ▼ ▼ ▼ ▼ ▼ ▼ ▼ ▼ ▼ ▼ ▼

Mississippi, 1830

On September 27, 1830, a Treaty was signed at Dancing Rabbit Creek, Mississippi, calling for the removal of the Choctaws to Indian Territory (Oklahoma). The journey was to begin in the spring of 1831, allowing the Choctaws time to arrange their affairs. In some communities white settlers, eager for the best farmland, initiated a campaign to burn homes and drive Choctaws into the woods. The winter of 1830-1831 was the most severe yet recorded and Choctaw casualties were high.

I REMEMBER MOTHER.

I remember once when I was a little baby lying on my back in bed. This is my first memory. Mother leaned over me and her long hair fell on my face. I grabbed it and pulled hard. My fingers were strong. She blew on my face to make me stop. I jumped and I almost cried. I must have looked really funny with my mouth wide open and my eyes big in surprise. I didn't know she could do that.

Then something in her eyes let me know she was making a joke with me. Nobody had ever done that before. She smiled and I giggled. Then we both giggled. I pulled on her hair and she blew in my face again. Over and over we played this funny game.

Then a shadow fell across us. My mother looked up. It was my father. I was afraid of him. He was strong and I was afraid of him. It was years before I would realize that his strength was there to protect us.

But I remember Mother.

I remember the day my father came in too early from hunting. He said, "We must move."

A Choctaw farm scene, pounding corn with a mortar, early 1900's

"We must move," my mother said. "We must move! What is 'We must move?' You better move back to the woods and bring me something to cook! 'We must move!'" She laughed.

"No," my father said. "A treaty has been signed. We must move."

I don't know what they said after that. My father took her by the arm and they went to their room. He closed the big door behind them and they spoke in whispers.

It was almost sundown when they came out again. My mother had been crying.

"Come with me," she said. We walked into the woods. Little Dog came with us, wagging his stubby tail.

"Where are we going? I am hungry," I told her. She kept walking.

Finally we came to where two old men were leaning against a tree. It was a red oak tree with wrinkled bark. While we watched, the men took their shirts off and started rubbing their backs against the tree. They rubbed and rubbed until their backs were bleeding. My mother took my hand and pulled me away.

"What are they doing?" I said. My mother kept walking.

We walked to the river and there an old man and woman were sitting in the shallow water. They dug handfuls of mud from the river. We stood in the bushes and watched. They were wiping the mud on each other's faces. They were crying and smearing each other with mud.

"Mother," I said, "why are these people doing these things? They are acting crazy."

My mother didn't say anything. She led me by the hand to another place on the river. There we saw several women with their dresses rolled up above their knees. They were crawling on the river stones. I had crawled on these stones before, once when I fell in the river. It hurt! These women were crawling on their bare knees.

"Mother, what is happening? What are these old people doing?"

"They are saying good-bye to their home," she said.

"They live in town. Their homes are in town."

"No, that is their house," she said. "Their houses are in town. These people are saying good-bye to their home." That is what my mother told me. "They are saying good-bye to their home."

I didn't know anything else about it till the next morning. It was still dark and I was sound asleep. Something woke me up and I smelled a burning smell. It smelled bad. I opened my eyes and saw that it was my hair. My hair was on fire.

I smothered myself with my pillow and wrapped a blanket on my hair till it stopped burning. Hot ashes started falling on my bed. When I looked up, the ceiling was on fire. I ran to the door and opened it. Flames and smoke shot into my room.

I dove into the flames and ran through the house. Soon I was standing in the front yard with my mother and father and big brother. Little Dog sat at my feet whimpering. We stood watching our house burn.

My big brother ran to the neighbor's house, to see if they could help us put the fire out. When he opened their door, smoke came pouring out. Their house was on fire, too. We ran inside and woke everybody up.

Before long, everybody in town was standing in the yards and watching their houses burn. The church and school were burning, too.

I heard guns firing from the church, not too far away.

"Run!" my father said. "Hurry!" He grabbed me and put me over his shoulder. We ran to the woods. Men came riding on horseback, firing rifles at the people watching their houses burn.

That is when it really started, the walking.

We hid in the bushes. When the men on horses came close, my father pushed my face in the mud. I held my breath and didn't move. When I couldn't breathe, I shook my head and my father let me up. He didn't say anything. I knew to be quiet. Little Dog curled up under my night-shirt, still as a sleeping baby.

That is how it began, the walking. It was hiding by day and *okla nowa*, people walking, by night.

We walked deep into the swamp where the horses wouldn't go. We waded through the swamp water to a small island. When we found a clearing in the center of the island, my father said, "We can settle here."

My father built a lean-to. He built the frame of river

cane and covered it with pine and cedar branches. My big brother and I helped him lift and lean the frame against a big cypress tree. This was our new home. Other families from our town made their way to the clearing and built lean-tos. We made a new village.

We hunted for squirrels and possums, but I couldn't eat much. My father wouldn't let us build a cooking fire. "We don't want anyone to know we are here," he said. We dug a hole and smoked the possum, but it was too tough to eat.

I woke up one morning and the air was frozen quiet. The silent snow had fallen overnight. It was very beautiful, with the lean-tos making gray shadows and shapes on the white snow. The green cedar branches hung low to the ground, covered with snow.

That was the morning we heard the wooden wagon wheels. The swamp was frozen solid and the horses could cross the ice. Everyone ran outside and we listened to the wagon wheels turning and crunching in the icy *misha-sopokni* snow. The sound echoed through the swamp and we were afraid.

We ran inside our lean-tos and hid. Blue-coated soldiers on horses drove the wagons into the center of the clearing. Nobody moved for a long time.

Moving the cedar branches, we saw the soldiers unloading stacks of blankets. We were so cold. All we had to wear was what we had gone to bed with the night our houses burned. The soldiers had blankets and they were passing them out.

There were blankets for the old people, blankets for the babies, blankets for everybody! When I tried to run and get my blanket, my mother pulled me back inside.

"We don't need their blankets," she said, stroking my hair. "We don't need their blankets." When my big brother tried to run to the wagons, she pulled him back, too. "We don't need their blankets," my mother said.

Years later, I would ask myself, "How could she know that before these blankets were passed out, they were deliberately infected with smallpox?"

The people began to die.

Those of us still living made our way through the swamp to a road on the other side. We found hundreds of people walking—*okla nowa*, people walking. The soldiers were riding horses and wagons and the people were walking.

"We are going to a new home," they said, "one they cannot take away from us."

We joined these people walking—my mother and father, my big brother, Little Dog and I. We walked by day and camped by the roadside by night. We built fires and huddled together with our feet close to the fire.

Every morning when we rose we sang "*Shilombish Holitopa Ma.*" It is "Amazing Grace," and the missionaries had taught this song to us.

Shilombish holitopa ma
Ish minti pulla cha
Hatak ilbasha pia ha
Ishpi yukpa lashke.

One morning I stood too long in one place on the icy road. The soles of my feet froze and stuck to the earth. When I lifted them to walk, the skin tore and my feet began to bleed. I tried walking on the sides of my feet, then my heels, but I was falling farther and farther behind. I limped into camp that night an hour after everyone else.

My feet were tough from running barefoot, but the new skin was tender. The next day blisters formed. A woman with a baby girl saw my feet when I warmed them by the fire. She tore strips of the baby's blanket for me to wrap around my feet. This worked for two days and I could walk better.

Then one morning the blisters popped. Heavy snow fell that day. I looked behind me and saw that I was leaving dark red footprints in the snow. My father waited for me to catch up to him. He crouched down to me.

"Son, you cannot keep your eyes on the bloody footprints you have left behind you," he said. "You must keep your eyes on where you are going."

I looked at the hills and woods in front of me after that. I could walk easier. The blisters healed and I could keep up with everyone else. We were once again *okla nowa*, people walking—together.

One morning the woman with the baby couldn't wake her little girl up. She wrapped her tight and covered her face with the blanket. She was crying while she walked, carrying her baby girl and crying.

The next day I saw the horses veering away from the woman carrying the baby. I said to my mother, "Why are the horses moving away from the woman with the baby?"

"That little girl has died," my mother said. "Her mother is carrying her to be buried close to her new home. Her baby girl died."

A week later, the woman fell on the road. Her baby rolled to the ground and out of the blanket. The woman tried to pick her baby up, but she couldn't stand with her baby. She was too weak. My mother ran to help the woman to her feet.

"Let me carry your baby," she said. When I moved to help her, my mother said, "You stay away! Go back with your brother. I will do this."

A few days later, my mother fell. It was early evening. We made our camp and built the fire. My mother slept with her feet facing the fire. That was the night I first felt the touch.

I was sleeping when I felt it. It was a cold touch, moving across my face. I opened my eyes and saw a shadow standing by the fire. It motioned to me and I followed it to the woods. Little Dog leapt up to go with me, but when he saw the shadow, he crawled back under the blanket, moaning in a deep dog voice. When we were away from the light of the fire, I saw it wasn't a shadow. It was my mother.

I went to her and wrapped my arms around her waist. She was cold and my arms went right through her. I stepped back and looked at her. It wasn't my mother. It was her *shilombish*, my mother's spirit. My mother had died and this was her *shilombish*.

"It's *hoke*," she said. "It's *hoke*. Only the bones."

I didn't know what she meant. She led me back to the camp and sang me to sleep.

The next morning my father woke me up with his cries. He was kneeling by my mother and pulling at his hair and crying. Women circled her and they were singing the wailing songs.

We lifted my mother and carried her as we went walking—*okla nowa*, people walking. My father carried her for most of the morning. Then my big brother carried her head and shoulders over his back while I carried her feet. She was heavy and I knew we could never make the walk this way.

The next night I felt the touch again. I knew what it was this time. I followed my mother's *shilombish* into the woods. When we were deep in the woods, she said, "You have to carry my body here."

"The panther will find you," I said.

"It's *hoke*," she said. "Only the bones." She made me drag her body into the woods. "Only the bones," she said. Then we returned to the camp. The fire was smoking embers. My eyes grew heavy looking at the fire. My mother sang me to sleep.

The next morning, my father shook me awake. He was so mad. "Where did you take your mother?"

He had seen my footprints and the marks made by her dragging body. I led him and my big brother to my mother's body. When we got there, the panther had done his job. We saw only the bones.

We carried the bones to the river and washed them. The old women burned cedar in the fire and we smoked the bones. We wrapped them with a strip of cloth and made a bone bundle. Now we could carry my mother to our new home.

My father, my big brother and I traded carrying my mother's bone bundle as we went walking—*okla nowa*, people walking. When it was my time to carry my mother, I wrapped my arms around her. It was as if my mother's *shilombish* carried the bone bundle, too, lifting me along with it. My feet seemed to float along the road. It was my mother's bone bundle and me!

The hills flattened and we walked on roads that turned from brown to black.

We smelled the river long before we came to it. We knew this river. We had crossed this river long ago. *Misha sipi*, the old place. *Misha sopokni*, beyond old. That is what the old people say.

They gathered everyone together that night on a bluff overlooking the river. They sang a song I had never heard, but the old people knew it. My father sang it, also.

Hina ushi pisali
Bok chitto onali
Yayali. Yayali.

Walking down the narrow path
We saw the big water
We wept. We wept.

Just after midnight the horses circled us and drove us down the steep bluff and onto a big flat boat. There were already 50 people on the boat, Choctaws from other places. I thought the boat would tump over. It swayed back and forth, sending cold water splashing over everybody. The old women had just started their singing when the boat settled and dark men with long poles pushed us away from the shore.

We were in the deep river soon and all we could see of the shore was a thick cloud of white fog. There was no room for the dogs on the boat. We were all so crowded and huddled together. The river was fast and wider than any river I had ever seen. We floated downstream before we started crossing. I sat between my father and big brother, holding on tight to mother's bone bundle. I knew I would never cross this river again. Once we crossed this river, we would never go back. Then I realized I would never see Little Dog again.

All of the dogs on the shore must have thought the same thing. They started howling. Everybody looked to the fog. The dogs howled and cried. They knew they would never see their people again.

Then I heard barking. It was Little Dog. He had jumped in the river and was swimming after us! I heard him over all the other dogs. I knew it was Little Dog. Then I saw him, coming out of the fog cloud. He was twisting and rolling like a small tree limb in the current. He was yelping and trying to swim to the boat. I couldn't let him drown. I stood up and ran to the rail.

"Little Dog!" I shouted. "Over here, Little Dog!" A big woman pushed me away from the rail.

"We don't have food for people. No dogs on the boat!" she said. She waved her cane over the rail and hit Little Dog on the nose. He sank into the black water.

I crawled under the rail and jumped overboard. I still was holding my mother's bone bundle. I knew it would float and keep me from drowning.

I saw Little Dog trying to swim, but the current was turning him around and carrying him away from the boat. I reached out for him, but the woman hit him again, this time on the side of the head. I saw Little Dog go under. I reached for him with both hands and my mother's bone bundle swirled away.

I watched it roll and bob in the waves. My mother's white, white bones were beautiful, dancing and twirling on the dark water. I let my arms go limp. I wanted to be in the river with my mother. I wanted to grab her hair and pull hard and feel her blow on my face. We could both giggle then. She doesn't smile at me anymore. She doesn't see how cold I am without her.

My father took the cane from the woman. "That is my son," he said to her.

He hooked me under the collar and dragged me from the river. When he lifted me from the water, I felt the cold air bite into my skin. I imagined I was a naked baby lying in the snow—a naked baby whose mother had already frozen to death. I was crawling over her, moving my tiny cold fingers across her face. I was trying to shape her white face into a smile. She opened her eyes and I was almost with her.

"Breathe!" my father shouted. I was so cold I was forgetting to breathe. He wrapped a blanket around me.

Then I remembered Little Dog. At first I was afraid for

him, afraid that he had drowned. But I know, still today I know it, that he did not. I know that by the time our boat reached the shore, a good family had fished him out of the water. They saw him from the riverbanks and fished him out. They didn't have a dog. By sunrise the next morning, Little Dog was running and sniffing in the woods around his new home. I know this, too. Little Dog missed me, but he was happy.

I laughed out loud to think of Little Dog.

"Little Dog is *hoke*," I said. I opened my eyes and I was looking at the buttons of my father's shirt. He was holding me.

"Yes," he said, "Little Dog is *hoke*. My son is *hoke*, too." My father was crying, smiling and crying.

When the boat landed on the other shore, everyone crowded onto the narrow plank. Someone pushed me from behind and I fell into the river. It was shallow and I could stand up. The water was just below my chest.

As I waded to the shore, I saw a little blue turtle, *luksi okchako*. It was floating on a small raft about 20 yards upstream. The turtle blinked at me and dove into the river. When it jumped, it pushed the raft to me. I waited till the raft floated up and bumped me on the chest. It was my mother's bone bundle, come home to me.

I grabbed ahold of a dead willow tree and pulled myself out of the river. The water soaked my clothes, but I had my mother's bone bundle again and the cold didn't sting so bad. I used the bone bundle as my pillow that night.

The next morning I found my big brother and my father and we went walking—*okla nowa*, people walking. We walked for days and days. I was very weak. I could not keep food down me since that night in the river.

Then we crossed another river and everyone fell down on their hands and knees. They grabbed handfuls of red dirt—the dirt here was red—and flung it to the sky.

"This is our home," they said. "We are home. This is our home."

Two days later we found the land that would be our home. It was a valley surrounded by rolling hills. A cold-water creek flowed across the valley.

The first thing we did was to build a wooden platform on a small hill, a place to lay mother's bone bundle before we buried it. I could not help them build it. I was too weak. But I did carry my mother's bone bundle to the platform when it was finished. They let me carry it.

One morning I woke up and I felt stronger than I had ever felt in my life. My father and big brother were carrying another bundle to the platform. It was wrapped in a blanket. I ran to help, but they did not look at me. They just walked on, looking at the ground. My brother was crying.

"I can help," I said, but they just walked on. When they reached the platform, they laid the bundle on it and started unrolling the blanket.

Then I felt the touch again. This time it was a warm touch, a warm-as-flowing-honey touch. I looked up and saw my mother. It was my mother, not her *shilombish*. It was my mother.

"You have come home," she said.

I looked at my father. He was kneeling by the platform, unrolling the blanket.

"You have come home to me," my mother said.

I looked back at the platform. My body rolled out of the blanket and came to a stop next to my mother's bone bundle. I was *shilombish*.

"No," I said. I wanted to go to my body, to wake my body up. Then my father looked to the spot where I was standing.

"Son," he said, "you cannot keep your eyes on the bloody footprints you have left behind you. You must keep your eyes on where you are going. You are going home."

My mother smiled at me and said, "You are home with me now."

Big brother in the story grew to be a man and they called him John Carnes. He had a son named John Goode, who had a daughter named Minnie Ochetama Goode. She was my grandmother. She had a son named Archie Tingle, Junior, who was born in Indian Territory before the family moved to Pasadena, Texas. He was my father.

There is a mound called Ninah Waiyah, just north of Philadelphia, Mississippi. Choctaws call it the Mother Mound. A simple wooden staircase leads to the summit of that mound. At the foot of the steps is a carved wooden sign that marks this as the origin site of the Choctaw people.

Beneath that sign grow blackberry vines. I know because I planted them years ago. I used to go back several times a year and with water from a nearby creek water those vines. But they do not need my watering any more. Their roots, you see, go very deep.

I remember Mother.

ℬONES ON
THE BRAZOS

▼ ▼ ▼ ▼ ▼ ▼ ▼ ▼ ▼ ▼ ▼ ▼ ▼ ▼ ▼

Texas, 1858

Master, which is the great commandment in the law?
Jesus said unto him, "Thou shalt love the Lord thy
God with all thy heart, and with all thy soul, and
with all thy mind. This is the first and great command-
ment. And the second is like unto it, Thou shalt love
thy neighbor as thyself. On these two commandments
hang all the law and the prophets."

—MATTHEW 22. 36-40 (KING JAMES)

Sometimes a story appears in such a way that you become con-
vinced the story found you, rather than the other way around. Such
is the case with "Bones On The Brazos." In the spring of 1991, I
was strolling through the small cemetery at Fort Belnap, Texas,
when I ran across the name Major Robert S. Neighbors, carved on a
granite tombstone. I was vaguely familiar with Neighbors as an offi-
cial who led an Indian exodus out of Texas before the Civil War.
The curator of the museum told me Major Neighbors had been
gunned down at the fort. My curiosity was sufficiently aroused.

Two months later I was performing in the History Department
at Texas A&M University in Commerce, Texas. I asked my host,

Dr. Ty Cashion, if he knew anything of Major Neighbors. As luck would have it, Dr. Cashion was editing the private journal of a schoolmaster stationed at Fort Belnap during Major Neighbors' time as Indian agent there. He allowed me to borrow the manuscript, which supplied the historical details of the following story.

Times of peace flow like a lazy river. You don't really notice them till they're gone. In 1858, on the clear fork of the Brazos River, peaceful people lived and farmed and sent their children to a one-room schoolhouse. They were Indian people, 2,500 all told. Major Robert S. Neighbors, Indian agent to those people, was the best friend they ever had.

One of the best friends of the Neighbors family was an old Choctaw man called simply Tom. He'd been farming there for 20 years and had a big family. The womenfolk in that Choctaw clan knew medicine, old medicine, herb-gathering, chant-singing, tea-boiling medicine. They were the first to be called upon, by whites and Indians alike, for a birthing or a curing, for in those days, "Love thy neighbor" also meant "Help thy neighbor." So it was only natural that a neighbor, a white man, would come to Tom asking for help.

"Tom, I've got a bear killing my livestock. I know you're a good tracker and a fine shot. Will you come help me get that bear?"

"Be glad to help," Tom said. Well, they never shot that bear. But when Tom returned home, he found his family shot up, massacred.

Now, I'd like to tell you they never found the men responsible for that crime. But they did. Less than a week later a new newspaper appeared in Weatherford, Texas, called simply "The White Man." It named the killers, among them the newspaper's owner, who proclaimed he would do it again, and again, and again—until the "red menace" was gone from the state of Texas. He called for volunteers and an army was raised. Those lazy times of peace on the clear fork of the Brazos River were gone.

But we are amazing, we humans, we are so resilient. Even in hard times, we will find our moments of joy. And as she did her work, inside and outside their small cabin, Ann Neighbors found her joy. She liked to dance and sing as she worked, and that's what she was doing when her husband, Major Neighbors, returned home with the news of Choctaw Tom.

When Robert Neighbors entered their little cabin, he carried with him a black cloud of sorrow. "Stop your dancing, Ann. Choctaw Tom's family has been killed," he said.

As Ann listened to the story, she moved her chair next to Robert's. When he finished and slumped forward, weeping into his hands, she held him and began to hum and rock. What they did next, you couldn't really call it dancing. But you couldn't call it not dancing, either.

Finally lifting his face, Neighbors saw his children huddled in the doorway, watching them. Throwing his hands up in the air, Major Robert S. Neighbors slid down off the chair, right there on the floor in front of the fireplace, and his loving family crawled all over him.

News soon arrived that an army of 500 vigilantes was approaching the Indian reserve to "clean up the place." They vowed they would kill anybody who remained, Indian or white. Out of fear, now, the settlement pulled in. Ranchers left livestock in the barn. Farmers left crops in the field. Merchants were overrun with people needing a place to sleep. Major Neighbors sought permission of the federal government to lead the Indians to the safety of Oklahoma.

Major Robert S. Neighbors (1815–1859) from a daguerrotype, circa 1851

All the while, Ann guarded over her family as only a mother can.

Returning home one night from a trip to Austin, well past midnight, Major Neighbors slipped quietly through the front door, hoping not to wake anybody. Ann was waiting up for him. Over steaming coffee, she told him of activities at the Fort while he was gone.

About three a.m., little Katy woke them up, standing by the bed. "Daddy, I have to go. Bad." Neighbors followed her outside, then saw her freeze before the door of the wooden outhouse.

"Daddy, there is somebody standing by the tree." Neighbors reached for where his gun should be, then realized he'd left it inside.

"Who is there?" he called out.

"Just me, Choctaw Tom," came the reply.

"What are you doing here, Tom?"

"Don't pay me no mind, Major. I'm just looking on your family."

"Tom, you need to be with your own family," Neighbors said, then wished he hadn't.

"I don't have a family, Major. But if you don't mind, I'd like to look on yours."

"Thank you, Tom. I'm much obliged. Now, Katy, finish up. It'll be fine."

Late that summer over 2,000 people, led by Major Neighbors, crossed the Red River to the safety of Oklahoma. They left behind their farms and most of their livestock to the people who drove them out. The day after the crossing, Major Neighbors sent a telegram, one copy to Washington, one copy to Ann:

I have this day crossed all Indians out of the heathen land. If you want a full description of our Exodus, see the

Bible, where the children of Israel crossed the Red Sea.

Major Neighbors' only task now was to return home and remove his family from the deserted Indian reserve. On his way home, he stopped off at Fort Belnap. As he entered a hardware store to pay a few bills, a man stepped in front of him to block his path. He heard his name called from behind him.

"Neighbors!" He felt a blow to his back, a hard blow, though he seemed not to move. It was the room that moved, all around him. As he fell forward, he saw shiny pink flecks on the shirt of the man in front of him, pieces of his lungs. When he hit the floor, a spasm flipped him over and he stared into the bitter face of a man holding a shotgun. The man spat upon him, but to Major Neighbors it was warm summer rain.

He was back on the hilltop on the day he and Ann selected the spot where they would build their cabin. When it started to rain, they covered themselves with the quilt they had spread their picnic on, but on a whim they both threw the quilt aside. They looked up into the sky and let the warm summer rain bathe their faces. Major Neighbors closed his eyes to feel it, smiled, and then he died.

When a neighbor told her the news of her husband, Ann was leaning over the fireplace, coaxing a cooking fire to life. An hour later the neighbor finally left her alone, sitting in her chair. Ann whispered aloud a feeling that would linger in her bones for a long, long time.

"Somehow," she said, "I did this to you." It made no sense, but then grief rarely does. Ann Neighbors stood up slowly and looked to the vacant doorway. Then, wrapping herself in her own arms, she began to dance. The loneliness would come later.

His tombstone reads simply Major Robert S. Neighbors. But Mrs. Neighbors and you and I, we know he was more than that. He was a spirit dancer, and to the descendants of those Indian people that he saved, his bones on the Brazos are still dancing.

ALEB

▼ ▼ ▼ ▼ ▼ ▼ ▼ ▼ ▼ ▼ ▼ ▼ ▼ ▼

Alabama, 1876

During the War Of 1812, fifty Mississippi Choctaw warriors sided with the Creeks and the British, going against the will of Choctaw Chief Pushmataha. After the war, these men were sentenced to death for treason. They and their families fled to Mobile Bay, Alabama. The modern-day Alabama Choctaws are descendants of those exiled Choctaws. My gratitude goes to Jay MacAlvain and Tom Wheelus for the following story, which includes much material from their family histories.

C ALEB LIVED IN THE DEEP WOODS, where things occurred we don't even have the names for anymore. When he was six, Caleb watched a rattlesnake charm a squirrel. He saw that squirrel screaming and chattering and running up and down a tree trunk. Caleb sat quietly in a clump of bushes, wondering at first why the squirrel was acting so strange. Then he spotted the rattlesnake at the base of the tree trunk, bobbing and weaving.

Soon the snake started his eerie whirring music, shaking his rattler behind him, his cold black eyes revealing nothing. The squirrel seemed drawn to the sound. Little by little he came closer, still screaming, still twitching his nervous tail. This went on for a long while, till even Caleb was rocking to the sound of the rattlesnake. The squirrel kept creeping closer and closer—till the rattlesnake popped the squirrel. Caleb jumped in shock at the speed of it. He sat watching, his own jaw dropped open, as the rattlesnake swallowed the squirrel whole.

When he was eight, Caleb saw his daddy do the same thing, charming a squirrel down a tree with a gourd rattle. His daddy didn't know he was watching, hiding in the underbrush and watching him rock and hum and shake his soft rattle. When the squirrel came close, Daddy Zeke reached out and grabbed it. He cut its neck so quick Caleb never saw him toss the dead squirrel into a bag hanging from his belt.

1876. Near Mobile Bay. Alabama Choctaw, Caleb was. He was ten when this story rolled around. Caleb had his little twin sisters, Robbie and Ruth, his Momma Tillie and his Daddy Zeke. Caleb also had his dream—once a week and sometimes more. He dreamed of creeping on soft cat paws to cold water springing right out of the ground, then flicking his tongue to drink, like a cat drinks, "Tck, tck, tck, tck, tck."

They were a happy family, living near two dozen other Choctaw families in the thick Alabama woods. Deer was plentiful and gardening was easy. The water from their well was clean and cold.

But there were weeping times, too. These were pioneer days and things were tougher then.

One night Caleb started crying and shaking. When he woke up, he was in his mother's arms.

"It's all right, son," she said. "Everything is all right, my sweet Caleb."

Caleb gradually stopped crying.

Under mother's watchful eye, a Choctaw family poses on the front porch,
circa 1904

"Momma," he said, "if you see a little cat in the woods tomorrow, will you give it some milk? It might be me."

"Caleb, I'm always gonna be there when you need me. And that cat of yours, he'll be there when you need him."

"Like Daddy with the squirrels?"

"What are you talking about?" Tillie asked.

"I saw Daddy talking with the squirrels."

"You saw him. Oh, Caleb, sometimes I think you see too much. Sometimes I think you see in the dark."

"Sometimes I do, Momma," Caleb said.

"Go on to sleep, now."

"*Hoke. Hoke*, Momma. I will be there for you, too. If you need me, I'll be there for you, too."

The next morning, little Robbie met the snake. It was a pretty spring day. From the ceiling hung a spider, dangling from a thread. Up by the house stood the hide-n-seek tree, surrounded by children.

Tillie sat on the back porch doing laundry, stirring and dipping the boiling pot.

Ruth was "it" and she was counting, "*Achufa, tuklo, tukchena*, one, two, three." Caleb and Robbie went running and hiding. Caleb dashed to the woods. Robbie ran to the porch, sneaking around the boiling pot.

"Go way, now," said Tillie. "Fire will get you like a snake, girl. Go on away!"

"Five, six, seven," Ruth counted.

Soon as Tillie turned her back, there was Robbie again, creeping behind the boiling pot.

"Eight, nine, ten! Ready or not, here I come!" shouted Ruth.

But the snake in the flames, it was ready, too. It snapped ahold of little Robbie's dress and wouldn't let go.

Before Robbie knew it, she was wrapped in flames, turning and twisting and running around the yard. The snake was curling and hissing. When Tillie and Caleb reached Robbie, her skin was wrinkled and black and she looked like a tiny ancient one.

For days, Tillie sat on the porch in her rocking chair, holding her baby Robbie, rocking and singing. But her baby girl was gone. By the time Tillie reached her, her baby was already gone. But Tillie kept on singing her healing song.

Chisus okut chi hoyo hosh.
Uba minti ula tok.
Chisno feyna chi hoyo hosh.
Ant falamut ia tok.

She wouldn't let anybody else touch Robbie. Three days went by and Zeke had to feed Tillie with a spoon. Then late one night, with lightning flashing and the thunderhead blowing up and rain pouring down, Zeke pried his little girl's black stiff body right out of Tillie's arms.

Through it all, Tillie shed not a single tear.

A soft wind rose the day they buried Robbie. It was a pretty spring day. A little breeze came up and lifted Tillie's hair. Zeke smiled to see it, but Tillie wouldn't allow any smiling.

"Never forget, Zeke," she said, "that same sweet breeze—that breath of God—that lifts my lock of hair, carries also in its unseen palm the ashes of my child. We have to go, Zeke. We have to move."

"Where to, Tillie?"

"Choctaw country, Indian Territory. That would be good. The snake took over here. We have to move."

"Tillie," said Zeke, "we'll never see this place again."

"Does that look like it bothers me, Zeke?" Tillie replied.

Four days hence, with their wagon packed, everybody climbed on, bound for Choctaw country.

When the slow rolling creaking of the wagon finally settled into a rhythm, Tillie looked back, and Caleb looked, too. Tillie saw the future, the front door hanging catywompers on one hinge, weeds sprouting through the floor, fat rodents nesting in the rafters. Caleb saw the past. He heard his sister's laughter—Robbie's laughter—raining through the leaves of the hide-and-seek tree.

From that day till the day he died, whenever he thought of home, Caleb saw that house. It was the only place little Robbie ever lived, and it was home to the hide-and-seek tree.

Thus began the long trip of one heavy day after another, praying for rain when the sun beat down, praying for the sun when the rain wouldn't stop. All the way to Memphis,

*An introspective and intelligent young Choctaw man,
C. H. P. James of McAlester, Indian Territory*

and all the way, Caleb dreamed, creeping on cat paws to the spring, and drinking as a cat drinks, "Tck, tck, tck, tck, tck."

Now, Memphis was a city. These Choctaws had never seen a city, never been bumped on a sidewalk, never had people look at them and laugh, never known the meanness of hurry.

Near sundown they looked out over the wide expanse of the Mississippi, waiting to cross on a barge. For the price of the crossing, Zeke had agreed to help some others on the trip, seeing as how they'd never been to the deep woods.

As Zeke stepped to the barge, a strong arm gripped his wrist and whirled him around. Zeke looked down at a skinny old man with his hat pulled low. Lifting the brim of the man's hat, Zeke saw only empty eye sockets. The man was blind. The muscles of his face twitched in a way Zeke knew.

The man grabbed Zeke by the collar, and said, "In your hour of greatest need, ask and you shall receive. Look to your friends in the trees. Look to the squirrels."

"Who are you?" said Zeke. The man pulled his hat low over his face and curled up into himself, saying nothing.

As he stepped on the barge, Zeke thought, "It was less like the man knew about squirrels and more like the man was a squirrel."

On the barge, Tillie caught a powdery perfume smell and looked up at a woman in a yellow dress and light green bonnet. "Your son looks to be the same age as my Jonathan," the woman said. She pointed to a boy leaning dangerously over the rail. "See, that's my son. I so love to dress him in blue. What color are your boy's eyes?"

Tillie was ashamed to talk her dull-sounding talk.

"No matter, I know who you are," the woman said. "My name is Constance and you are Tillie. My husband already told me. I know your husband, too. His name is Zeke. My husband tells me you're to help us, you and your family. We are so obliged. Did I say pleased to meet you? Well, I am." And saying that, she walked away.

Tillie sneaked a look at Jonathan. She saw he wore his hair in ringlets. He held his chin in a cocky way. "We will help them for the price of a crossing," thought Tillie. "How much for the price of a crossing?"

So cross they did and to the woods they went, driving that old rugged cross of a Choctaw wagon, following two factory models owned by the family of young Jonathan, smartly dressed Jonathan, riding his pony like a prince Jonathan.

Zeke soon learned that "help us out a bit" meant a little more than that. It meant setting up camp, stalking and hunting, and cooking the game, and all the other chores that qualified as work.

While the Choctaws walked, the others rode. Young Jonathan, ever-braver Jonathan, he'd begin every morning circling the camp, popping his pony with a buggy whip. "Strike like a snake," he'd say. Tillie shivered every time he said it.

They were a week into the woods when they first heard the panther call. Sitting by the evening fire, they heard the panther call. Nobody said a word, but that night Caleb's dream came stronger than ever before.

The next morning, Zeke gave Caleb the reins.

"I'll get an early start on the hunting," he said. "Just take it easy. I won't be far. Holler if you need help."

Ruth sat beside him as he drove. They had traveled less than a mile when Caleb heard a noise off to his left. He turned to see Jonathan, smart-riding Jonathan, circling and popping his buggy whip. Closer and closer came Jonathan, till, CRACCKKK—he cut Ruth's face with the whip!

"Snake cracks like fire!" he cried, then rode away.

Caleb pulled Ruth over to him. He put her face right up against his cheek. Her whole body shook and her tears were flowing. As he held her, as he caught the scent of his own family blood, something happened to Caleb. The bristling began.

What had brewed and bubbled and waited all these years now had its way with Caleb. His dream came to life and he clicked his tongue like a cat drinking water, "Tck, tck, tck, tck, tck." What lived and breathed inside him was no little boy, not any more. He had left that little boy on the back porch of the house by the hide-and-seek tree. What lived inside him now was no housecat, no full-grown cat nor kitty, neither one.

It was instead the panther. The porch and wagon were gone, only the forest remained. And surveying his new domain, through the glassy dark glint of his eye, sat Caleb. On the wooden seat of a wagon headed west he sat, staring at the disappearing pony of his prey.

Now everything waited only for the sun to go down.

At the evening meal, when the smell of boiled pork and the whisper of the flames called all, all came—all but Jonathan. He was still riding his pony, as if he knew his fate that night. It was well after dark, and young Jonathan was still riding in the woods. Deeper and deeper he went.

"What happened to your cheek?" asked Tillie, seeing the cut on Ruth's face. Both families sat by the open campfire.

"Where could Jonathan be?" said Constance.

"You are bleeding!" said Tillie, moving to get a closer look at Ruth.

"Will that boy never learn?" asked Constance.

"You have to cover your face against the tree limbs," said Tillie.

"We'll just have to save him a bowl," said Constance.

"Take care of your face," said Tillie. "You could poke an eye out. You could go blind!"

"But it'll get cold," said Constance.

Caleb rose and walked quickly into the woods.

"Now Caleb, where you going?" cried Tillie.

"He's *hoke*," said Ruth. "He knows the woods."

You best believe Caleb knew the woods, while wider and wider, deeper and deeper, went Jonathan.

Caleb had walked less than 100 yards when he felt the twitching of his back muscles, like a horse getting rid of a fly. Knowing he couldn't stop it, Caleb was afraid. His chest heaved and he felt like a giant was ripping him apart in a rhythm. Finally, his knees buckled and his mind went blank.

When Caleb opened his eyes, he could see in the dark. He could see himself creeping on soft paws to cold water springing right out of the ground. He leaned to the water and drank, "Tck, tck, tck, tck, tck."

Lifting his face and twitching his nose, Caleb caught the scent of a pony—and the sweat of a boy. The pony smelled the panther, too, and reared back, sending Jonathan crashing to the ground. As he lay immobile, the breath knocked out of him, the cold clammy fear of death took over that boy. A minute later he leapt to his feet and took off running, pumping his arms, breathing in gulps of chilly night air. But his speed was no match for the panther.

The next morning, long before the morning star cast its silver hope on a deep blue sky, Caleb awakened. Long before the pony, bereft of rider, returned to camp, Caleb awakened. Long before they found the boy shaking and bawling by a sumac bush, Caleb awakened. Long before Constance held her son close, long before she saw blood in Jonathan's hair, long before she wadded up her dress to stop the bleeding, long before all that—Caleb awakened.

Caleb awakened and lay shivering, running his tongue across the dried blood coagulating on his lips. Caleb stared at the dark streaks on his overalls. Trembling like a fawn, he slipped his balled-up fist into his left front pocket. He opened his hand just wide enough to wrap his fingers around the still-warm flesh of Jonathan's ear.

But even before that, Tillie awakened and instantly

knew everything. For she was a good mother, and a good mother knows. If her child lies, a good mother knows. If her child takes as his own the possessions of another, a good mother knows. And if her first-born son is off in the woods, shape-shifting and devouring the neighborhood children, a good mother just knows.

Being a good mother, Tillie knew exactly what to do. She went comforting another mother. Finding Constance sitting in her wagon crying, her boy now sleeping beside her, Tillie said, "He'll be fine, that boy of yours. You are lucky you still have your boy."

"I do not feel lucky," said Constance. "I envy you, Tillie. How close you all are. Your family is so full of love for each other."

"We are close but we hurt," Tillie said. "I lost my baby, my girl Robbie. She burned up. She died, wheezing her last breath, right in my arms. That's why we left Alabama."

When Constance pulled her close, Tillie started crying, like she never did with Zeke. Slow at first, as if feeling her way at it, Tillie started crying. In a moment she was sobbing with every piece of herself—crying and crying and crying.

That was the last talk they had, Constance and Tillie. But from that talk, Constance had made a decision. The next morning, her family turned their wagons around and headed back home to Memphis. From that talk, Tillie had made a decision, too. She had decided to fight to keep her Caleb.

"Zeke," she said after the others had gone, "you get us to the river."

"Tillie, that's ten miles away," said Zeke.

"Zeke, get us there tonight. We have to leave here, get as far away from here as we can."

Even with the late start, they made the river by nightfall. Everybody turned in early that night.

About one o'clock in the morning, Tillie rose from her sleeping pallet and quietly dressed.

"I will be back," she said to Zeke. "Promise me you will stay right here. Promise me that."

"I promise," he said. "Where are you going?"

Tillie didn't answer. She climbed from the wagon and walked out of the moonlight and into the dark of the trees. She leaned up against a tree and unrolled her apron. On her lap lay her butcher knife. Tillie picked it up and drew a deep cut in the flesh of her thumb.

Dark thick drops fell to the ground. Then Tillie started walking, and as she walked, she shook her hand and flung fresh blood on the floor of the woods, on the trees and bushes. Every step she took, she flung blood in random wet splotches. But her steps were not random. Tillie was going to the river.

When she reached the riverbank, she paused only long enough to gather her dress to her waist before she fell forward on her knees. The mud was cold and she knew the water must be, too. But Tillie crawled right in, catching air in her dress. She looked like a bubble floating on the water. Wading out to the middle of the river, Tillie waited.

The river was green and soft cypress limbs stretched ten feet over the water. Tillie tiptoed, bobbing up and down, gently floating. The moon was dancing yellow on the water.

"*Chisus okut chi hoyo hosh*," she sang. It was her healing song. "*Uba minti ula tok*."

On the banks of the river she saw two green eyes, shining and peering through the ferns. She went on singing.

"*Chisno feyna chi hoyo hosh*." The black purple coat of the panther shone in the night. It was a sight to see, dark velvet rippling in the moonlight. Still she sang.

"*Ant falamut ia tok.*" It was her Caleb—it was the panther—dipping his shivering paw to test the water. Easing himself into the river, gliding like a water moccasin, coming to his momma's call, it was her Caleb.

With every stroke of a leg, with every twitch of an ear, black fur began to recede. The paw of the panther became the palm of a boy. Cat claw untwisted into finger. With Momma Tillie calling, singing her song, Caleb was coming home.

The story should be over here. We should be drawing to a happy conclusion—our story of a child, once strayed, returning to his rightful ways. That would be the western way, but this is a Choctaw tale—and something happened that would change everything.

For the first time in their marriage, Zeke broke a promise. He woke up asking himself, "Where did she go?" Dressing quickly, he climbed out of the wagon. Zeke followed what he hoped were Tillie's footprints, as best he could see them in the filtered moonlight, to the base of a tree. There he spotted the butcher knife.

"Oh no, please," he said. "Where did you go, bleeding so bad? Woman, you can't be in the woods bleeding. That cat will sniff you out!"

He grabbed his rifle and his gourd rattle. Remembering she had insisted on making it to the river, he ran in that direction. Zeke dove through the woods, slapping branches with his free arm. The forest was thick, and the deeper he went into it, the more the darkness seemed alive. He was glad he had his rattle.

Caleb was still swimming—now halfway to his Momma—when Zeke saw them both in the green waters of the river, the panther and his Tillie. He balanced his rifle on a cypress branch and reached into his belt bag for the rattle. In the soft pocket of fog floating on the river, the sound of the seeds shifting in the rattle seemed to come from everywhere. The panther froze. Tillie stopped her singing.

It should have been an easy shot, the way he'd lined the rifle, pointed right at the spot where the shoulder blades met the neck. But Zeke started shaking like never before. He knew his Tillie lived or died by this one shot.

Then everything was drenched in sweat, hot sweat, flowing from every pore. Zeke was sopping wet and tears came squirting from his eyes.

"This will not happen," he said. He wiped the sweat from his eyes, took a deep breath, and cast a true, sweet aim at the panther, curling his finger around the trigger. Then Zeke heard a chattering in the tree limb just above his head. He looked up to see a squirrel. "Help me," he pleaded.

"Ask and you shall receive." That was the promise—and did he ever.

At that moment hundreds of squirrels came raining down from the trees, pounding his head, knocking his gun to the ground, and him, too. The next thing he knew, Zeke was laying face first in the dirt, looking up and wondering aloud, "What plague of locusts looking like squirrels has descended on me now?"

When he pushed the squirrels away and rose to his knees, he looked to the river and saw the most beautiful mother and child the world has ever seen. It was his Tillie holding his Caleb, alive as ever living be.

Zeke crawled to the bank and lifted Tillie and limp-bodied Caleb from the river. There they sat, rocking like triplets in a watery womb, till the dawn came burning its way through the blue.

Two months later, they made their crossing, as so many

Choctaws had before them—taking the boats at Memphis, braving the wilds of Arkansas—then making their homes in Indian Territory, present day Oklahoma.

Zeke and Tillie built their home way off deep in the woods from anybody else. But times were hard and a decade later fever took Zeke and his beloved Tillie.

By this time, Ruth had married and moved away, but Caleb never married. As people began to populate Choctaw country, he moved deeper into the woods. He lived this way, real quiet-like, for years.

Then, well into his eighties, Caleb joined a community church. He'd come walking in from the woods every Sunday about the time the service was beginning. He was always welcome at church socials.

Folks would say, "That Caleb, he's all right. Have you ever noticed, no matter how scarce game is, no matter how bad hunting is in these parts, it doesn't bother Caleb? He can always be counted on to show up with a batch of good fresh meat. Yessir! You can always count on Caleb."

$\mathcal{T}$HE CHOCTAW WAY

▼ ▼ ▼ ▼ ▼ ▼ ▼ ▼ ▼ ▼ ▼ ▼ ▼ ▼ ▼

Oklahoma, 1892

Several years ago I was walking shoulder-to-shoulder with an older Choctaw gentleman on a 21-mile reenactment of the Trail of Tears. Hundreds of Choctaws had come together to commemorate the journey our ancestors had survived in spite of incredible hardships. As we crossed over the Arkansas River into Oklahoma, the man grew silent. I grew concerned, for it was a hot day and a long walk for an older man. I studied him closely and he seemed to draw into himself. Then he started humming and finally, in an ancient, gravelly voice, he began to sing a burial hymn.

Farther along, we'll know all about it,
Farther along, we will understand why.
Cheer up my brother, live in the sunshine.
We'll understand it, all bye and bye.

When he glanced up and saw me staring at him, he said, by way of explaining, "We just passed the cane place and I was thinking about Willie Frazier."
"I don't know Willie Frazier," I said. He looked at me in sur-

prise and proceeded to tell me the story of a man who was execut-
ed the Choctaw way, an ancient code of justice. This was before
courtrooms, jails, or prisons; it was a way of honor, drummed in
stone in the heartbeat of the Choctaw people.

The story began with a dispute over ownership of a pony. One man picked up a fence stake and another a stone the size of a grapefruit. When that fight was over, Willie Frazier stood holding a stone dripping with blood, and a young man with a cracked skull lay at his feet.

And the sun set and the night was cold and dark, but the
sun rose again in the morning.

The next morning, Willie walked the five miles to the tribal council to tell them news they already knew. The moccasin telegraph, or Indian gossip, travels fast with news of a killing. The sentence Willie was given came as no surprise, for it was clearly written in Choctaw law that if you took a life, you gave your own in its place. Willie was also given a burlap bag filled with thirty pieces of river cane, cane cut to the size of a man's thumb. The cane was for counting, one stick for each day he had remaining in his life. He was to bury a piece of cane each morning and when the bag was empty, return voluntarily to the tribal council for his execution.

On his way home that day Willie thought of Tobias, a young orphan boy he had taken to raise. He called him in from the woods and that evening, on the green grassy slope overlooking their little white frame house, they buried the first piece of cane.

And the sun set and the night was cold and dark, but the
sun rose again in the morning.

The next day, following the burial of a piece of cane, Willie took Tobias down to the river. They sat quietly in the underbrush, watching *loksi okchako*, a little blue turtle, sitting on the edge of the water. In a short while, a young bobcat came sauntering out of the woods. He spotted *loksi*, crept cautiously to it, then slapped the turtle on the side of the shell. Right away, the turtle drew in. As they watched, the bobcat kept slapping, leaping back and slapping again, till finally the turtle rolled topsy-turvy over and into the water and swam away.

Willie picked Tobias up and on the way home told him, "Son, it's very important in life to know when to pull in and when to fight." Tobias nodded.

And the sun set and the night was cold and dark, but the sun rose again in the morning.

Every day began the same, with the burial of a piece of cane, and a new lesson for Tobias in the Choctaw way. One day, after their quiet ritual, the clinging and clanging of the church bells told the boy it was Sunday morning, Day Seven.

Following the singing and the sermonizing at the little log church in the woods, Willie spoke softly to Tobias on the way home. He put his arm on the boy's shoulder and said, "Son, I'm a simple man where religion is concerned. As best I can tell, there are really only two words that matter. The first of these words is Hallelujah! It's a happy sound. You hear how the preacher, how the whole congregation shouts it out. Hallelujah! It's a happy sound, a praising sound."

Willie stopped and turned to face Tobias. "But the second word, son, is more serious. It's Amen! and it means *so be it*. Amen, Tobias, means *I'm for it*. He paused and looked deep into the boy's eyes. "Son, don't ever cast your Amen! vote unless you're willing to pay for it." Tobias nodded.

And the sun set and the night was cold and dark, but the sun rose again in the morning.

Day Thirteen, Willie told the boy about Ninah Waiyah, the Choctaw sacred mound near Philadelphia, Mississippi. He said, "All Choctaws must go to that place, at least once in their lives, to see the ground we all came from. It shows respect for our people and will keep us strong and happy."

Tobias looked up at Willie and said, "Pawpaw, will you take me there?"

"No, son. I have already been. But you must take your children there someday." Tobias nodded.

And the sun set and the night was cold and dark, but the sun rose again in the morning.

Day Twenty, Willie felt the burlap bag growing lighter. He knew that soon the nightriders would come to pay him a visit. These were convicted American felons who haunted Indian Territory, where federal law had no authority. They often sought out Choctaw killers to tempt them with the taste of life, if they would join their gang.

That evening, under cover of pounding rain, eight men tied their horses to Willie's porch rail. They kicked down his door to make a point, but were disappointed to see only an old man and a young boy. While Willie cooked them coffee on the stove top and served them around the table, he listened to their leader tell him, "You can come along. We need a night watch and a cook. But that boy's too young, he cain't come. He got to stay behind."

When Willie turned them down, the men grew angry. They pushed their chairs away from the table, then stood and surrounded Willie. Tobias, watching from his chair by the stove, thought the men were going to beat his pawpaw. But Willie looked at each of them with a strong gaze till they slowly filed out the door.

Just before stepping outside, the last of the outlaws turned around, picked up the edge of the table and lifted it up to his chest, dumping all of the contents into Willie's lap, including the scalding coffee he had just poured for them. As Willie sat still and felt the burning liquid blister through the denim, he watched his last hope for life walk out the door.

"Do you remember the lesson?" he said to Tobias.

"Yes," said the boy. "It's very important in life to know when to pull in and when to fight." Willie nodded.

And the sun set and the night was cold and dark, but the sun rose again in the morning.

Day Twenty-eight, the church gave a special service for Willie Frazier, since it would be the last one he could attend. The service closed with a verse from Willie's favorite hymn.

Faithful till death, sayeth our one loving master.
A few more days to labor and wait.
Toils of the world will then seem as nothing,
As we sweep through the beautiful gate.

On the way home, Tobias looked up at Willie and said, "Pawpaw, I saw you crying in church."

"Huh," said Willie. "Bug flew in my eye."

"It's *hoke*, Pawpaw," said the boy. "Same bug flew in my eye." Willie nodded.

And the sun set and the night was cold and dark, but the sun rose again in the morning.

And the sun finally rose on the eve of the final day. Willie and Tobias did nothing special that day. They spent most of the day walking in the woods, listening and looking. Willie pointed out a small red fox. Tobias spotted a mother skunk with her babies. That evening they cooked a simple meal of corn soup, cooked it outside over a campfire. Tobias listened to the sizzling crackle of dried leaves as he dropped them on the fire and smelled the fresh aroma of burning pine.

Willie went to bed early, but he tossed and turned and couldn't sleep at all. About three a.m., he heard a knocking on his windowpane. He sat up and glanced through the smoky glass. In the moonlight, he saw his sister and a stranger on horseback, leading a horse with no rider.

He cracked open the window and his sister whisper-hissed through it. "Willie Frazier, you hard-headed Choctaw, you listen to me. We took up a collection, Willie. I have a gift for you, the gift of life. This man can get you down river. He has a boat there. There's enough money for you to get to New Orleans. You can go anywhere. Now come on, Willie."

Willie didn't hesitate. He moved to the door and shut it quietly. He lifted the window high and leaned out into the damp night air.

"Sister, it's right nice of you folks to take up a collection for me, but listen here. This boy I keep with me, Tobias, I've been teaching him the Choctaw way. He is sound asleep now, but he is very smart boy. He'll know what it means if I am gone. This time tomorrow, if I'm not in the ground, all those lessons I've been teaching him are blown away. Now you tell all those folks that Willie appreciates what they trying to do. But that gift you want to give me, that gift of life, it's not yours to give. Go on home now. Seem to me you up past your bedtime."

Willie's sister did not reply. She sat on her horse for a long moment, staring at her big brother. As he moved to shut the window, she turned to go, knowing it did no good to argue with Willie Frazier.

"Oh, sister," Willie called after her. "You are right about one thing."

"What?"

"This here Willie Frazier is one hardheaded Choctaw! You got that right. Willie Frazier is one hard-headed Choctaw."

He shut the window laughing, he crawled into bed laughing, and he pulled the quilt up over himself, still laughing. Willie Frazier laughed himself to sleep that night, and he slept like a baby. He was awakened by the sound of a distant rooster, crowing in the dark before the dawn, as the sun rose on the final day.

During the burial of the last piece of cane, as they raked their fingers over the red *Okla Homma* dirt, Willie told Tobias of the Choctaw code of honor, of the value of a man's word. Then he told him of the penalty for a killing, and what he had done and what he must do.

"If you want to see me," Willie said, "come down to the graveyard and press your face so close to the ground that your breath moves the grass like wind as you speak, and I will hear you."

On his way to the tribal council, Willie dropped Tobias off at his sister's place. As he turned to go, the boy pulled him by the shirttail.

"Pawpaw, don't make me go to the graveyard to see you. I don't want to go there."

Willie knelt down and held Tobias close for the final time. He pressed the boy's head against his chest so the boy could listen to his heartbeat as he told him, "Come to the cane place. That is where my spirit will be."

The last execution following the traditional Choctaw Code of Honor was that of Silon Lewis on November 5, 1894.

As Tobias stood in the doorway and watched Willie walk away, he stretched his arms wide and pressed his palms against the doorframe. When he felt his arms begin to weaken, he pressed harder, then he tensed every muscle in his body. He stood on tiptoe and tilted his head back, staring at the blue morning sky. He closed his eyes and squeezed them tight shut. His body began to shake and he gulped in a lungful of air and held his breath until he heard it.

A rifle cracked and sent its sound echoing down through the cottonwoods in the river bottom, sending its bullet right through the heart of Willie Frazier. The boy slumped over for a long, sad moment. Then he felt a breeze, a strong breeze, blowing his hair and lifting his arms to the sky. He cried out, in as strong a voice as he could muster, "Amen!" as he cast his vote for the way of honor, for the Choctaw way. Tobias and Willie, they were willing to pay for it.

With the old man's story over, we returned once again to the hot asphalt road and the Trail of Tears walking.

"I'm gonna sing it again," the gentleman said. "This time I am singing for everybody, living or dead, that ever walked that road of honor, that *hina achukma*." His voice was tired and cracking, but his song was a sweet lullaby.

> Farther along, we'll know all about it,
> Farther along, we will understand why.
> Cheer up my brother, live in the sunshine.
> We'll understand it, all bye and bye.

$\mathcal{B}$ROTHERS

▼ ▼ ▼ ▼ ▼ ▼ ▼ ▼ ▼ ▼ ▼ ▼ ▼ ▼ ▼

Oklahoma, 1900

As they began to establish communities in Indian Territory (Oklahoma) following the Trail of Tears, the Choctaws first built Christian churches. Missionaries, predominantly Methodist and Presbyterian, had established the churches as the center of Choctaw townships in Mississippi. In the years that followed the Removal from Mississippi of 1830–1835, many Oklahoma Choctaw communities, though Christian, were isolated from the outside world, speaking only Choctaw.

JOSEPH HOTABEE WAS A CHILD of the morning. He appeared in the morning, then 20 years later made his departure, walking over a mountain and vanishing in the light of the morning sun.

Joseph was a left-behind, one too many mouths to feed for a pioneer family passing through the Kiamichi River Valley. His first day with the Hotabees began as the light of dawn cast a soft glow over the snow-covered valley. Momma Hotabee opened the door and found him on the doorstep, wrapped in the tattered remains of a quilt. The stuffing was gone and Joseph's straw-colored hair poked through a blue star in the quilt's design. When she pulled the quilt from his face, she saw a baby pale as death.

"He won't last the day," thought Momma. She brushed her hand across his hair. It was full of cockleburs.

She told the neighbors across the street about the dying baby and they spread the word across the valley. At the noon hour, 200 Choctaws gathered at the one-room church to sing and pray for the baby's soul. It was a strange gathering. The Hotabees were oddly proud and the crowd's mood was as much curious as mournful. They stayed till dark, then said what they thought were their last good-byes to the unfortunate child. But even as they filed out of the church and walked to their horses and wagons, many people stopped and turned to face the church, now turning a deep pink in the sunset—as if they expected something more to occur.

Momma Hotabee always assumed, as did every one else in the valley, that she was the first Choctaw to ever lay eyes on Joseph. They were all wrong in this assumption. Billy Hotabee was the first Choctaw to see Joseph. Billy was two years old when Joseph appeared.

Sleeping next to the window in the living room, Billy woke up when he heard the wagon pull to a stop 20 yards down the road from the Hotabee house. He lifted himself up and rested his chin on the windowsill. He saw the horses stomp and snort and he watched their smoky breath disappear in the chilly predawn.

Billy saw Joseph's father—Joseph's real father—climb awkwardly down from the wagon and deposit the bundle on the Hotabee doorstep. Billy saw a thin-faced woman, her eyes red-rimmed from a night of crying, look back as the wagon pulled away.

"She is his mother," thought Billy, "and she is leaving him."

It was after midnight when Billy first saw his new

brother up close. He had lingered near the altar at church as everyone prayed over Joseph, but he never really looked at him.

But now, after midnight, the Hotabee household was sound asleep, and Joseph's next feeding would not occur till two a.m. Billy pulled on his britches and quietly tiptoed to the kitchen. He slid open a drawer and, too short to see, felt for the wooden handle of the butcher knife.

Carrying the heavy knife with both hands, he crept out the back door. Billy wore no shirt and, as he stepped into the night air, his skin prickled in goose bumps. He walked cautiously to the cane break some hundred yards to the rear of the house and sat down in the wet mud amidst the tall river cane. He gripped a length of cane with his right hand and hacked away at the base of the stalk with the butcher knife.

Twenty minutes later, Billy stood by the crib where Joseph lay sleeping. His father's snores vibrated through the walls and Billy shivered slightly in the cold, dark house. He reached through the bars and touched Joseph lightly on the face. Joseph's lips pursed into a kiss and he began a sucking motion. Billy lifted the quilt from Joseph and saw his fat white belly and the dried curl of umbilical cord extending from it.

Billy held a foot-long piece of cane by his side. He ran his thumb over the sharp point he had carved on the tip, much as he had seen his father do when testing the sharpness of his ax. He touched Joseph on the belly with the stick, gently at first. Joseph made a mouth noise and increased the speed of his sucking. Billy pulled the cane back, six inches from Joseph, then jabbed him hard in the side just below the ribs.

Billy pretended to sleep through the ensuing uproar, as his father searched every corner of the house for the rat his mother was convinced had bitten Joseph.

The next morning Momma Hotabee noticed the mud stain on the seat of Billy's britches, but her mind was too cluttered with excitement to make the necessary connections. Billy was safe.

When Joseph—after several feedings with milk from the Hotabee cow—survived the night, many believed they had witnessed a miracle. They even pointed to the strange wound on his side as a mark of the spirit. A week later, when the pale baby was still alive, everyone in the valley was convinced the community had been divinely selected to receive this blessing of a baby.

They were well into their second week of showering the baby with special gifts when a passing Chickasaw man stopped in town to water and feed his horses. He was quickly ushered to the Hotabee household to behold the dying miracle baby. The house was already packed by the time he reached it. He was, after all, the first outsider to witness their miracle.

The crowd of townspeople was focused in a corner of the living room, where Joseph's crib had been moved for the occasion of the viewing. The Choctaws parted and formed an aisle when the stranger approached. As he leaned carefully over the rail, Momma Hotabee removed the quilt from the baby's face. He looked at the baby and his eyes grew wide. He looked at Momma Hotabee, then back at the baby. He felt the baby's forehead. His eyes grew wider and a nervous look crossed his face. Clearing his throat, the stranger turned to face 30 anxious Choctaws waiting for him to speak.

"There's nothing wrong with this baby," he said. "He isn't going to die. He is a white baby. There are thousands just like him living outside this valley."

The crowd stood stunned and silent, for they had never

seen a white baby. Momma Hotabee peered into her child's blue eyes. "Anyone can see this baby is a miracle," she whispered. But no one was looking at the baby. They were all staring at the stranger, unwilling to have their miracle so easily dismissed.

"But his hair!" they shouted, standing on tiptoes and pointing to the crib. "Look at his hair!"

"Yes," he said, patiently waiting for the clamoring to subside. "It is yellow hair. Many white people have yellow hair."

"Very strange people, these white people," they said, nodding to one another.

"You can say that again," the Chickasaw replied.

And so they did.

"Very strange people, these white people."

But people are stubborn. Once someone has determined that something is a miracle, or that something is inherently evil, that thought will never go away. Such was the case with Joseph. He seemed to bask in the glow of anticipated miracles.

As the brothers—for that is how they were seen—grew older, Billy took to the woods. He spent most of his day hunting for small game with a blowdart gun he had made by hollowing out a three-foot length of cane. After breakfast each day, Billy would dash to the piney woods behind the house before he could be given any chores, while Joseph stayed behind to help his father.

By the time he was 12, Billy had become a skilled hunter, often catching rabbit or squirrel for the evening meal. Joseph, meanwhile, grew to a stature far beyond his years. Though he was thin, he was taller than his older brother. His father took pride in the way Joseph could fell a small tree and cut firewood.

A lone white face—an adopted child or offspring of a mixed-blood marriage—stands out during lunchtime at Riverside Indian School, 1901.

One evening, Billy was late for supper and the family began eating without him. A steady rain had drenched the valley and Joseph had spent the day in the barn, learning how to cut shingles from his father. Time was drawing near for the annual duty of repairing the roofs of the gravehouses behind the church.

When Billy finally appeared on the back porch, his clothes were soaking wet and he was covered with mud.

"Don't come in till you clean up!" his father shouted. Billy grinned and held up three fat rabbits by the ears.

"It took me all day, but look what I caught!" he said. "I had to lay still for hours to catch all three of 'em."

"Clean yourself up! It's hard to tell who's the wild animal, you or those rabbits," his father said.

Billy's mother brought him a clean shirt and pants. He stripped and stood in the back yard, washing himself in the rainfall. When he was dressed and seated at the table, his father ignored him.

"You should see Joseph work," he said. "He cut a dozen shingles, each one the same thickness. They'll look good on the gravehouses."

That night a norther blew in and Momma rose to put another log in the woodstove. She cracked open the back door to see if ice was forming on the tree limbs. The rain made a slick whispering sound. She was startled by a sound at her feet and turned to see Billy sitting on the back porch, curled up in a quilt and watching the sleet.

She carried him inside and made coffee. His face had a dazed look. When she set the cup in front of him, he wrapped both hands around it to warm himself. The steam rose from his cup.

"We will clean and cook your rabbits for breakfast," Momma said. Billy sat up and looked around the kitchen as if awakening from a dream. He sipped his coffee and nodded.

"They are good fat rabbits."

"I know," said Momma Hotabee. "I'll fry them. They will be a good breakfast on a cold morning."

Joseph continued to grow. "Like a beanstalk," his mother would say, and by the time he was twelve he was almost as tall as his father. Billy was stout and strong, and his hunting trips now lasted for several days. He kept the Hotabees and several neighboring households supplied with deer.

The family always celebrated the two brothers' birthdays on the same day in late spring, as nobody knew when Joseph was born. For Billy's fourteenth, and Joseph's twelfth, the neighbors slaughtered a hog, and most of the town was invited. They made a long table in the back yard by placing planks on sawhorses and covered it with dishes of corn soup, potatoes, grape dumplings, and frybread. The smell of sizzling fat arose from platters piled high with thick slabs of pork steak. Momma Hotabee's deep-dish blackberry cobbler was featured for dessert. Everyone served themselves and sat wherever they could.

When the meal was over, Mister Hotabee went to his room and returned with his gift for Billy. It was wrapped in a square of shiny, worn leather. "Here, son. You can put this to good use," he said. "It belonged to my father."

Billy unrolled the leather and held aloft a knife with a foot-long blade. Its handle was carved from a deer antler. Billy, shy in the gaze of the crowd, hung his head and clutched the knife to his belly. His father touched him on the shoulder and returned to the house.

Billy kept his head down and mumbled thank you a dozen times as family friends came by to wish him happy birthday. He held the knife out and a few men took it from him and held the blade to the light to admire it.

Billy thought they were all gone when he heard a deep voice behind him say, "Hope to see you in church tomorrow." He turned to see an older friend of his father's. Billy looked at his own shoes till the man walked away. He hadn't been to church in over a month.

Billy looked up to see his father approach Joseph and hand him a cedar box.

"This belonged to my grandfather, the first Hotabee to come over from Mississippi. Happy birthday, son." Joseph opened the box and took out a hatchet with a dull, silver-colored blade.

"It is heavy, but you are strong enough to use it. Sharpen it well and it will cut beautiful shingles," Hotabee said. "My grandfather's gravehouse could use a new roof."

Joseph was soon surrounded by well-wishers. He stood taller than most of the Choctaw men. With his shining yellow hair, he was like the sun in a friendly solar system, circled by moons and planets of friends. The women smiled and touched his sleeves. Some even brushed his blonde hair from his face.

"Look how tall you are."

"I would hate to have to keep you in clothes. You grow so fast!"

When Billy slipped away to the river, only Momma Hotabee noticed, watching him out of the corner of her eye.

Following church the next day, Joseph and his father wandered among the gravehouses, quietly planning their work. The gravehouses, 27 total, were neatly laid out behind the one-room church. They were eight feet deep, allowing for several bodies to be stacked upon each other, and they had no walls above the ground. A finely shingled roof adorned each of the houses. Their upkeep was a thing of great pride for the Choctaw families.

Every Sunday the townspeople would admire the work of Joseph and his father, as they kept the cemetery clean and the gravehouses shingled.

Billy retreated more and more to the woods. He cleared himself a campsite in the river bottom and slept outside in the cane break as often as he did indoors. "Cane Boy," the townsfolk came to call him. "Cane Boy Billy."

Though Momma Hotabee was the only one who saw it, a strange pattern of incidents occurred surrounding Joseph and his brother. Whenever Joseph would clean and shingle the gravehouse of a friend, he would, of course, receive their thanks and blessings. The next morning that same family would receive a generous portion of wild game, left by an unknown donor on their doorstep. Cane Boy Billy never heard the praise; that all went to his brother.

One Saturday morning, a group of elders from the church approached the Hotabee house. Joseph was by this time 20, his brother 22. Momma Hotabee had coaxed Billy to join the family for the day, so she could clean and mend his clothes. Billy sat near the stove in the living room, listening, while the elders spoke to his father on the porch.

"We have grown, Brother Hotabee, as a town and a church," said the spokesman. "We need a leader from our own, not a traveling preacher."

"I have seen that need," said Hotabee.

"He may not be ready. He is young. But your son is strong and a good man. We would like to ask him to be our preacher." Billy shook to hear those words.

"Someone knows," he thought. "Someone has seen my strength." Tears welled up in his eyes.

"You may ask him, if that is your wish," said Hotabee. He opened the door and the seven men crowded into the living room. Seeing Billy sitting by the stove, the spokesman said, "We have a question for you."

"Yes, what is it?" said Billy.

"Where is your brother? We have business with him." The seven men nodded as one. Billy pointed to the backyard. When the men had left the room, he gathered his dirty clothes and made his way quietly to the river bottom.

That night at the supper table, Mister Hotabee spoke too slowly, too deliberately—as if his words were steaming for release and he struggled to contain them. The brewing storm outside, the dark roar of the wind, echoed his words.

"He should be home! Billy should be here to share in the blessing his brother has brought on this family." He filled his plate then looked through the window as a flash of lightning lit up the backyard. A clap of thunder shook the house.

"They have asked me to talk tomorrow," said Joseph. "I don't know what to say."

"Where is your brother?" Hotabee asked. Had he looked up at the next crack of lightening, he would have seen Cane Boy Billy, or at least Billy's shadow. Billy was standing in the backyard, in the pouring down rain, watching his family share their last supper together. He was waving his deer-handled knife and cutting patches from his hair. He was crying in grief for what he planned to do.

"I am going to the church," said Joseph.

"The wind will blow you away," Momma Hotabee said. Joseph said nothing in reply. He put on his coat, pulled his hat low over his face, and quickly walked out the door.

Leaning into the gale, Joseph struggled the half mile to the church. It was pitch black inside the building and the lightening, now flashing several times a minute, cast yellow and blue squares on the walls. Joseph knelt at the altar and closed his eyes.

The wind whistled through cracks in the walls. Then the lightening and the wind and the rain ceased, only for a moment. But that moment was enough. For the first time in his life, Joseph Hotabee knew fear. He was crouched and kneeling in what should be for him the safest refuge in the world, and he was afraid. A strange copper taste filled his mouth and the hair stood up on his neck. Fear now had a face and Joseph knew it.

He saw before him a vision as clear as the cloth on the altar. Billy was walking down the center of the road, oblivious to the rain whipping around him. He was approaching the church and he was carrying Joseph's hatchet.

When Billy reached the church, he was bleeding from the scalp. He stood for a moment on the porch, then leaned into the door. Although there was no lock, only a simple

A tornado cuts a path through Indian Territory

hinge that turned inward, the door would not open. Unknown to Billy, Joseph leaned against it from the inside, his boot heels dug into the warped floorboards and the back of his head pressing against the oakwood door.

The full force of the gale returned. Billy thought he heard voices coming from the gravehouses.

"Where is your brother?" the voices sang, over and over. "Where is your brother?" Billy gripped the handle of the hatchet and swung it with all of his strength, burying the blade deep into the door. He turned and fled to the cane breaks.

Joseph felt the blow against the door. He touched the back of his head. It was bleeding. He stumbled to the altar, where Momma Hotabee found him the next morning. It was just after daybreak when she shook him awake, saying,

"We should get home and clean up. People should not see you like this."

The storm was now a low-hanging ceiling of clouds that dipped and teased the treetops. The light was a dark yellow color, and tiny whirlwinds seemed to rise from the earth itself, scattering leaves and branches. They leaned into each other, bracing against the wind, for the half-mile walk home. To her many questions, Joseph only said, "The storm was strong."

Momma Hotabee had clean pants and a white cotton shirt ready for Joseph in his room. She washed the dark stains from his scalp and neck, then left him alone, saying, "You can eat in a few minutes. People will be early at church today. You should go soon."

After a quick breakfast of cornbread and milk, Joseph picked up his Bible from his bedside table and—without looking back—left the Hotabee house for the final time.

Since he had last left the church, the sky had darkened and the clouds seemed alive. Debris floated in the air and was whisked away in short bursts of wind. As he neared the church, Joseph saw a large crowd mingling and talking in the red dirt yard by the front door. The few people who had entered the church now joined those in the yard, staring and pointing at the sky to the rear of the building.

Following their gaze, Joseph saw a dark tornado cloud moving in the direction of the church. It was ripping up trees and everything else in its path.

What happened next flew by in a matter of moments, though to the Choctaws present it all seemed as slow moving and inevitable as a boulder rolling down a bald mountain.

A cry, at first a single cry, emerged from the earth, a giant ripping cry. Soon a hundred voices groaned and sobbed. A word here and there could be distinguished. Names, the voices were calling names—Choctaw names, names of people standing in the yard, names of those buried in the gravehouses.

The sound was coming from the graveyard. The people saw nails twisting over the church, nails ripped from the gravehouse roofs. Boards joined the nails, lifting to the sky. Then came the bones, moving in a strange and beautiful dance. Everyone wept to see the beauty of the dance. Some bones were recently buried. They were brown and yellow. Other, older bones were white as chalk. The bones were calling to their families. They were singing. Families held each other close to hear the beauty of the song.

Then the singing stopped and a deep cry bellowed from the bowels of the tornado.

Everyone turned to Joseph. He looked to the door of the church and saw the hatchet. At that moment Joseph Hotabee knew why he was there and what he was to do. He strode to the church and pulled the hatchet from the door. As everyone knelt around him, praying for their lives, Joseph held the hatchet high and gripped the handle with both hands.

He turned his eyes to the tornado and with every fiber of strength in his lean body, Joseph flung the hatchet to the ground. With a long, deep exhale, the breathing, living wind fell silent.

The tornado split in half.

One small twister darted to the west of the church, while the other flew to the east. Small trees and dust rose from the woods on either side of the church, then settled to the ground.

Still dancing, the bones fell from the sky, returning to the graves from whence they came. The boards fell neatly into place on the gravehouse roofs. With soft pinging noises, the square head nails nestled into the same holes they had pierced some half a century ago.

The Choctaws stood as one and sang "*Shilombish Holitopa Ma*"—"Amazing Grace" in English.

Joseph picked the hatchet up and turned his eye to the east, to the tallest mountain, and started walking. He had barely walked a mile when he saw Billy standing in the middle of the road. Billy's arms hung loosely at his side, relaxed but ready. Joseph knew this posture from watching Billy stalk game.

As he walked to Billy, he saw the rough gaps in his hair, showing pieces of bloody scalp. Black circles surrounded his brother's eyes, eyes that looked wild and mistrustful. Joseph came closer and Billy shuffled his feet in preparation for a fight.

Joseph handed him the hatchet, bowed his head, and said, "Do what you must."

A moment later, a short breath left Joseph and the hatchet fell to the ground.

Billy clung to his brother, squeezing the air from his lungs. "Can you ever forgive me?" Billy sobbed as he spoke.

"I forgave you long ago," said Joseph. He cried also as he spoke. "You are a Hotabee, the oldest son, and I have brought you trouble. Try to forgive me. But more important still, forgive yourself."

Billy nodded and Joseph continued.

"Your people need you. You are Choctaw. Take this hatchet and begin to build. No one can do this but you."

The two brothers exhausted their strength that morning, holding each other. When finally they parted, Billy picked up the hatchet and walked back to his people. They say he preached a rousing sermon that day—the story of Cain and Abel.

With the hatchet and his new-found strength, William Hotabee, formerly Billy, began to build. He had seven sons and daughters, and they and their many offspring spread throughout the valley and beyond. Though they lived, as we all do, east of Eden, in the land of Nod, they learned to love each other, and in that love grew strong.

And Joseph Hotabee? Whatever happened to Joseph Hotabee? You already know about Joseph Hotabee.

Joseph Hotabee was a child of the morning. He appeared in the morning, then 20 years later made his departure, walking over a mountain and vanishing in the light of the morning sun.

$\mathscr{L}$IZBETH AND THE MADSTONE

▼ ▼ ▼ ▼ ▼ ▼ ▼ ▼ ▼ ▼ ▼ ▼ ▼ ▼ ▼

Oklahoma, 1908

Paul Cross, a Choctaw preacher from up near Emory, Texas, told me this story about his grandmother Lizbeth. He also told me this, "I've learned something about family, son. It can be your blood kin, but it don't have to be. It's the folks that love you, plain and simple. That's your family. And that's where you long to be, in good times or bad. You want to be with your family." This story is about family.

It was the time of *Luak Falaya*, the Long Fire, the fire that is never allowed to go out, all year long. When the year draws to a close and the embers burn low, a new fire is built, and the people of the village bring things—remembrances of quarrels they've had throughout the year. A letter, a fence stake, and these things are then laid upon the fire to be burned and blown away, as insignificant as the smoke of time. Enemies cling to each other and weep to think of what they have said and what they have done. The ashes from the old fire then ignite the new and the cycle begins afresh, in the time of *Luak Falaya*.

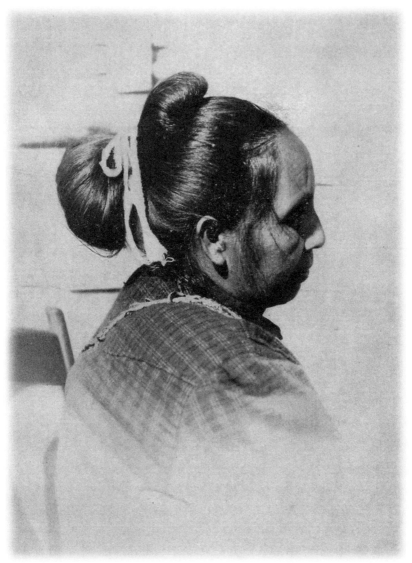

A Choctaw woman, Heleema, wearing the ancient hairdo, circa 1908

This story was meant to be told; and its telling moves to the early days of the last century, to the house of Lizbeth. It was an Old Testament summer. The trees were bare from the drought. The sycamore leaves lay thick and golden on the riverbank. They crackled and whispered back at you when you stepped on them. Lizbeth lived in a cabin overlooking the village, near the hollow where Blue Creek flowed. Her children were grown and gone, her husband had died, been bone-bundled and buried in the mound out back, leaving Lizbeth with only her dog Shob to keep her company. And the children of the village, they were always around, for they loved their Lizbeth.

For at Lizbeth's cabin, they never had to draw water, or chop firewood. And just who do you think performed these chores at the house of Lizbeth? Why, the children, of course. But they didn't have to. They did them because they loved their Lizbeth.

Now there were times when Lizbeth would close her eyes and shiver, then she'd lean back and call for her dog.

"Shooooob!"

The people'd say Shob would bound through those woods and 'fore you'd know it, he'd be sitting by her side. But the children said it different. They'd say Shob would just be there. In a flash, he was there.

Then one day Lizbeth called for Shob and he didn't right away come. She whispered to the boy Billy, "Shob's dead, Billy, laying back by the well. Drag him up to the porch for me. Then you and these other children, y'all run along home. I want to spend time with Shob."

For Lizbeth had long ago decided she wouldn't bury Shob in the backyard like a regular dog. No, she'd make a bone bundle out of him and bury him in the grave house, with family. But what she did next stirs up this story real good for us, for she didn't bury all the bones. She saved a thigh bone, and most any evening you could see her rocking in her chair—just whittling and rocking—carving a bone knife from her old dog Shob.

The people of the town, they'd say things like, "Oh, that Lizbeth. I don't know 'bout her. You can see her there, in the rocking chair, plain as day. But her mind, shure 'nuff, is somewhere else!"

The children began to stay away. Billy's Momma Rachel didn't like him up there, but she didn't forbid his going.

And change kept right on coming. Billy's father went for a week-long hunting trip to Arkansas. The river flooded. A month later his partners returned, saying he'd drowned, but they brought no body back. And Billy's Momma Rachel started to die a little bit, too, everyday. She began to die a little bit, too.

Then came the night three strangers rode to town. Least, two were riding; one was draped over his horse, dog bit and sick unto death with hydrophob—rabies. They went knocking and waking folks, saying, "We're looking for the healing woman, the woman with the madstone."

"Must mean Lizbeth. She live up the hill up yonder," someone said.

As the strangers climbed the hill, Billy was about ready to leave Lizbeth's for the evening when she began to shiver her chill.

"Wait, Billy. We got company coming. Why don't you stay here till they leave? Don't let 'em know you're here, but watch everything."

Short while, men knocked. Billy was already up in the loft, hid up under a quilt, barely breathing but keen-eyed watching. Lizbeth opened the door and told the men, "Bring him in and take off his shirt." On her hands and knees, she pried up a loose board from the floor, then she lifted a basket, small; and from it took a stone that looked like a persimmon.

Billy saw the bite marks on the man's arm—purple,

scabbed-over, pussing, swoll up big as Billy's leg. As Lizbeth moved the stone slowly to the wound, it seemed to glow. When it neared the man's arm, the stone leapt from her palm and nestled itself deep into the teeth marks. After while, it rattled to the floor and Lizbeth washed it in a milk bowl. Billy saw the milk turn green.

Seven times she brought forth the stone and seven times it buried itself in the ugly wound, till finally it lay still and shiny-black on the cabin floor. Billy lay quiet as the freeze.

"He'll get better, now," Lizbeth said. "You can take him, but don't sleep in the woods tonight. That dog may still be 'round."

The men left and Billy came down.

"What are you looking so for, Billy? It's no magic. It's a madstone, from the belly of a white deer. It will suck the venom from a rattlesnake bite, or the raby poison from a mad dog."

Lizbeth reached out to Billy and said, "You keep it now. There is a growing darkness in those woods. You going to need it. You best be going. Your Momma'll be worried about you. And something else, Billy."

"Yes, ma'am."

"Guard your secrets. They are your soul."

Once in the woods Billy felt that chill of darkness. Several times he saw shadows flitting by, but he stayed on that path, he kept moving steady on, and he was all right, for the dark still held its secret, but our little Billy held the stone.

'Bout time Billy come home, his momma was slicing through a lemon, sending that aroma all through the cabin, feeling its juice sting the cuts on her fingers. She didn't turn to look at Billy at all. Instead she picked up a spoon he'd come to call the pounding spoon, with a long wooden handle on it. What next transpired was a percussive thing, but it was no music Billy could understand. Rachel whacked that spoon on the lip of the basin, scraped that spoon on the back of a chair, slapped that spoon on the side of her leg, till Billy longed for a rhythm he could feel.

Had Rachel simply pounded her palm and shouted, "I do not want you there," that he could tolerate. Instead, she closed her eyes, gripped her own hair, and swooshed the spoon through the air, Billy dodging the flight of it. When finally she whacked it hard on the thick oaken table, Billy's surprise was not that the spoon didn't splinter and break, but rather that the table itself did not fall asunder.

"Do not go there," she said. "I will not have it." Billy took a step to go, then turned to face his mother.

"How much of it," he said, "how much of your anger is about me, and how much of it is about my father?"

Billy knew enough not to await an answer. And Rachel knew enough not to risk a reply. But Billy and his mother both fell asleep that night filled with love for each other, for it was exactly this wisdom of knowing when not to speak—that was their bond.

From that day till the day they died, whenever they caught a whiff of a lemon, they remembered that night. It was the night of Billy's manhood. It was the night they both realized his father had died.

When the daybreak sun rose, it moved like a deep purple bruise on the pink breast of morning. Billy went to chopping firewood, seeing as how *Luak Falaya* was only a few days away. Midmorning, he felt the chill and, for the first time, his bones were cold from the inside. Less than half an hour later, Billy heard a rustling sound from behind the woodpile, but when he went to look, there was only a pressed-down spot, like a deer leaves when it lays, or a dog.

Mid-afternoon the sun began to pale. Then a breeze came in like the rise and swell of a dark ocean. When the sky went black, Billy took off for Lizbeth's, running, running, knowing all the time that somewhere in the cracking leaves growing ever-so-close behind him, that somewhere in the cold breeze sending shivers down his spine, that somewhere in the darkness, a thing of evil lurched his way—his hour, so they say, come round at last.

It was slow and sketched in detail when it finally occurred. The snap of a twig, the lift of a gaze, and there stood the dog. It was a big dog, a dark dog with yellow eyes. Billy heard a low growl, like mean, sharp gravel in the air all around him. In a quick flicker, the dog knocked him to the ground, sank his fangs deep into Billy's shoulder, tugged at the flesh, flung high a rope of bloody foam, and then was gone.

Billy saw red flecks on his white muslin shirt, outlined in the shape of a dog's bite. When they grew to the size of pennies, he knew he must move. He crawled to the creek, ripped open his shirt, and bathed the wound. With his hand shaking, he slipped the stone from his pocket. It rolled across his palm of its own accord, then hovered for a moment as soft and sweet as a butterfly before settling into the warm pink of his skin. He shivered once to feel it, then fell into the deep fetal sleep of healing, a sleep which sent him reeling into light.

At daybreak, Billy and his Momma Rachel both began their final journey to the house of Lizbeth. Billy dragged himself within 50 yards of the cabin and slumped against a tree trunk. He couldn't go any further. Rachel, her pounding spoon in hand, blinded by her anger, strode past him on her way to Lizbeth's cabin. She struck the door once, hard, before Lizbeth opened it.

"Where is my son? You have him here."

"I didn't see him yesterday," said Lizbeth. "But you best find him. I 'spect that dog's still nearby."

Rachel stared at the old woman's eyes in accusation. She saw two soft flames begin to grow, and the next words Rachel more felt than heard as Lizbeth offered, "Blessed be they that mourn, for they shall be comforted. Go to your son, now. He needs you."

Rachel slowly backed down the porch steps and when she turned to the path, there stood the dog. Four long steps and it knocked the woman to the ground. From where he sat, Billy lifted his chin onto the tree stump. He saw the dog dip his dark muzzle to the woman's throat. There was a ripping sound and the black dog limped and lurched his way into the woods.

But the woman that dog pounced upon was not Billy's mother. The face those yellow eyes gazed into was not the face of Billy's mother, and the blood now splattering those leaves was not the blood of Rachel, Billy's mother. For Lizbeth had pushed Rachel aside, and it was she, Lizbeth, who now lay still as a broken bird.

Billy ran to Lizbeth and lifted her head onto his lap. She was soaked in blood from her chin to her waist. Billy's eyes filled with tears, and one fat tear rolled off the tip of his nose and splash-landed on the cheek of Lizbeth. Whereupon, she opened one eye, saying, "Is he gone yet?"

"Is he gone yet? What do you mean?" said Billy. "Are you dead and talking?"

"No," said Lizbeth, calmly brushing a strand of hair from her face. "I am not dead and talking. I am very much alive."

"But your dress? Look at your dress!"

"Oh, this old thang?" she said. "You like it?"

"No," said Billy. "Uh, yes. I like it fine. But it's bloody all over!"

"Oh, that," said Lizbeth. "I believe the blood must belong to that dog. You see, when he went for my throat, I went for his."

Then reaching into her apron pocket, Lizbeth pulled out the bone knife from her old dog Shob, saying, "I got there first! You see, it's not always the size of the dog in the fight. Uh-uh. Sometimes it's the sharpness of the knife at his throat."

They buried that dog where he died, 50 yards down the hill. Billy dug a hole, then kick-rolled him into it. As they were burying him, Rachel sidled up to Lizbeth, saying, "You could have been killed. You did that for me."

"I did," said Lizbeth. "And for that boy. He already lost a father. He didn't need to lose a mother, too."

Finally, after everything I've been telling you, came round the time of *Luak Falaya*, when the people cast their grievances to the flames. Just as they were about to light the new fire with ashes from the old, stepped forth Rachel. Onto the fire of the past, she laid the pounding spoon, then she turned to Lizbeth, saying, "You are too old to live alone. My husband, I know, will not be back. You come to live with us. My son and I need you. Come today. We can pick your things up later."

"I would like that," said Lizbeth. "But I want to bring Shob."

Rachel just shook her head. "You bring whatever you want."

"Ok," said Lizbeth. They still talk about what happened next, how that skinny little Choctaw woman threw back her head, puffed out her chest, and let fly with a cry loud enough to knock down death's door, calling out,

"Shooooooob!

And there he was, right by her side. It was a six-month old pup, but it was Shob. That very evening Lizbeth and Shob moved into the house of Rachel.

I would like to tell you they lived happily ever-living loving after, but life doesn't work that way, not with two women sharing the same kitchen. Before long they were arguing about whether the plumbing ought to be indoors or out. But I can promise you this. Those two widowed women and those two fresh pups lived together for many years, safe and warm in the love of family. May each and every one of you be so blessed.

$\mathcal{T}$ONY BYARS

▼ ▼ ▼ ▼ ▼ ▼ ▼ ▼ ▼ ▼ ▼ ▼ ▼ ▼ ▼

Oklahoma, 1936

The following narrative is based on an interview with Tony Byars, a full-blood Choctaw and graduate of both Jones Academy and Chilocco Indian School. In August of 1997, Byars was inducted into the "Wall of Fame" and honored as a distinguished alumnus of Jones Academy. He died less than a year after our interview, but he left behind a request that this story be told.

I have taken the liberty of making slight changes in the dialogue in the interests of language appropriateness. I have also changed the names of all characters with the exception of Tony Byars. The spirit of the story, however, remains intact. I am convinced Tony Byars would be pleased, and hopefully proud, that this version of his story is included in a volume of Choctaw tales.

TONY BYARS APPEARED TO ME in a story. I first met him at a spoken word coffeehouse performance in Austin, Texas. I was well into a story of the Choctaw Trail of Tears, closing my eyes and leaning into the microphone to focus on an old chant, a chant that was sung during that 1831 journey. Choctaw is not my native tongue, but those long nasal vowels are so beautiful to the ear, and I always feel that special crackling spirit-magic enter the space when they are sung.

When I opened my eyes, there was Tony, sitting at a previously empty table in front of the microphone. His head was nodding to the rhythm of the chant, tears were streaming down his face, and his lips were mouthing the words of the chant along with me:

Hinaushi pisali
Bok chitto, onali
Ya yali. Ya yali.

When the concert was over, I sought him out. This man, I knew, had a story to tell.

Two weeks later, Tony ushered me into the living room of his home in the mostly brick suburbs of north Austin.

Tony had attended both Jones Academy and Chilocco Indian Boarding Schools in Oklahoma. When he was eight, a man from the Bureau of Indian Affairs told his parents that life would be very difficult for them if Tony did not attend boarding school.

You can visit him on weekends, they were assured; he can come home for holidays. So, a few days later, Tony boarded a bus along with many other Indian children on their way to Jones Academy. It was seven years before he would see his family again.

When the bus arrived, everybody knew who Tony was. His big brother Sweeney Byars had fought on the boxing team at Jones Academy. In fact, as a member of the Jones Academy boxing team, the older Byars had won the Golden Gloves National Title. In 1936, Sweeney Byars would fight in Berlin, Germany, as a member of the United States Olympic team.

At first, the members of the boxing team were anxious to have another Byars join them. But when they saw how small Tony Byars was, their interest changed. Now, everyone at Jones Academy, especially the members of the boxing team, wanted to be known as the first boy to beat up Sweeney Byars' little brother. But Tony Byars had speed, and what he couldn't outfight, he could outrun.

Tony soon made many friends among the younger boys, and they nicknamed him "Chukfi," or "Rabbit" in Choctaw.

"Go fast, Chukfi," his friends would call to him. "Go fast!"

Tony's reading teacher, Miss Warner, was especially hard on the young Indian boys. Every Wednesday morning, she conducted a "spelling bee" in her class of twenty students.

"Everyone will now rise. This side of the class, line up against the windows. From over here, against the wall."

She loved her spelling bee. "You." She pointed to a full-blood Kiowa. "Spell the word DART."

A shy, older boy stepped forward, and his reply would become one of her favorite stories: "D-I-R-T."

"That is just about what you are worth. Now, please sit down."

Tony's best friend was Bobby Bluehorse, a boy his age. One Sunday, coming back from Chapel, they spotted a patch of cane growing in a streambed. After cutting several stalks, they fashioned blowguns out of the hollow cane, then climbed to the top of a silo. Tony filled his blowgun with corn while Bobby kept an eye out for victims. "You won't believe who's walkin' by," Bobby said.

Tony peered out the tiny opening and there, just below

the silo, walked Miss Warner, target side to the rear. Tony let fly a stream of corn kernels. Miss Warner flinched, but only once. Then she froze, still as a covey of quail, waiting for the hunter to make the next move.

Tony and Bobby leaned up against the wall of the silo, barely breathing, for the longest time—five, ten minutes. When they finally looked up, she was gone.

Bobby beamed. "Whoa! Sweeney Byars got nothing on you! Way to go, Chukfi! Way to go!"

That evening, the school administrator, Mr. Starks, called Tony into his office. "Are you familiar with the belt line, Tony? Have you heard the other boys talk about it?"

"No, sir."

"Well," said Starks, "by this time tomorrow, you will know all about it. Get a good night's sleep."

The next morning, Tony saw several of the "Big Boys" climbing up a willow tree, cutting switches and limbs. Then he spotted an older boy standing off away from the others, looking very quiet and serious. The boy was swinging a tree branch like a heavy baseball bat. With a loud unnh!, he swung the branch in a circle, so the fat end exploded from the ground up.

Watching the belt line form, with more than 100 students lined up on either side, Tony remembered Bobby's words from the night before. "Pick one side and run close to it, right under their arms, so neither side can get a good swing. Run low to the ground, and don't fall down. If you do, they'll be on top of you!"

Tony was ten steps down the line before he first felt the sting of leather belts slapping his face. Then came the switches, flailing his back till the skin cracked open. When the first big branch landed on his right shoulder, Tony staggered and felt his knees buckle.

Only Bobby's voice kept him going. "Go fast, Chukfi! Go fast!"

Tony's eyes were glued to the ground when he heard it. "Unhh!" He glanced up as the fat end of a willow bat caught him right between the eyes, standing Tony Byars straight up as 200 students of Jones Academy drew breath and waited for him to fall.

But Tony Byars did not fall, and the remaining blows fell on a body no longer able to feel them. When Tony slumped across the finish line, Bobby carried him to bed, and the long day soon blended into night.

The next morning, just before roll call, Miss Warner walked down the aisle and stood beside Tony.

"You know, you don't have to come to school today," she said.

Tony stood up, and—though he was still a good half-foot shorter than Miss Warner—he grew to meet her eyes.

"I see no reason not to come to school today."

From his easy chair in his living room, old man Tony Byars sat still for a long time. I knew this part of his story was over and I waited.

Finally, he continued. "No matter where you are, if you look hard enough, you can find one decent person." With that, he began to craft the most beautiful story I had ever heard.

I missed my family, but I never talked about it—we all missed our families. In the seven years I was at Jones Academy, I can count on the fingers of this hand the times I saw any family of any boys—not just mine. Nobody ever came.

When they told me my brother had died in a farm accident, that's when I missed my family the most. And when they told me I couldn't go home for the funeral, I felt more alone than I have ever felt in my life.

They say Mr. McDay, my English teacher, came up to see me that night. It was raining real hard. I didn't see him, but if he opened the door behind me he would have seen my face pressed against the cold, wet windowpane. He would have heard me singing.

Hinaushi pisali,
Bok chitto onali,
Ya yali—ya yali.

Walking down the narrow pathway,
We approached the Big Water,
We wept, we wept.

I think he was there. I think he sat outside my door, on the floor, leaning up against the door. I like to think he stayed there till the rain stopped and he heard me crawl into bed.

Next morning, Mr. McDay called the teachers together for a meeting in Mr. Stark's office. He said they shouldn't teach that day, out of respect for me and my brother.

Mr. Starks stood up and said, "We'll fire you. I'll fire you."

Then Mr. McDay stood up himself and said, "There is a sickness here. Right here, in Jones Academy. And whatever it is, it's going around and I think I've caught it. I'm just too sick to teach today."

Then Mr. Stark just stood there. He couldn't believe what happened next. One by one, every one of them teachers stood up. Every one of them started talking about having a little fever; one had a cough, another had a tummy ache. Finally, the entire faculty walked right out the door.

Classroom at Riverside Indian School, 1901

There was nobody but Mr. Starks and Miss Warner still in the room. And the way Miss Warner tells it, he looked down his nose at her and said, "At least you have good sense."

"Well," she says, "that just rankled me the wrong way. 'Mr. Starks,' I told him, 'that boy is strong, and he's a good boy. And me, I may have good sense, but I also have a splitting headache. I just can't teach today.'"

And she walked out the door. School was canceled that day. I spent the whole day fishing down at the lake with Mr. McDay. Mostly we just fished quiet-like, talking some about my brother, some about my family.

When the sun started to go down, I knew my brother was already buried and in the ground, or headed that way. I waded out in the water. The sun looked so pretty, like a big orange ball. Mr. McDay got up and walked behind a tree, like he didn't want to watch me. I wanted to do something for my brother before the sun went down. But I didn't know the right chants, what to do. I was only a boy, standing up to my chest in water, staring at the sun.

Washing clothes at Riverside Indian School, 1901

Up behind me Mr. McDay began rocking his head against the tree, mumbling words I still remember:

"It is like the thunder said.
He who was living is now dead.
We who were living are now dying.
If only there were water amongst the rock,
But there is no water.
Only dry sterile thunder without rain."

He was like a crazy man talking. I was standing chest-deep in water. It was *tashimbo* (crazy) talk. I was only a boy, trying to bury my brother. And there were no old women with long fingernails to pick the flesh from the bones. Not even a bone bundle to bury. Only dry, sterile thunder without rain.

I sang the only song I knew that was sad enough.

Hinaushi pisali,
Bok chitto onali,
Ya yali—ya yali.

I was only a boy. And the sun sinking into the lake. And my brother's body into the earth.

My brother was gone, but when I stepped out of the water that day, I stepped out a man. And I always remember, wherever you are, you can always find one decent person.

That's what Tony Byars said. After all that, that's what he said. As I stood on the sidewalk outside Tony Byars' house, he told me, "In two weeks, I'll be inducted into the 'Wall of Fame' at Jones Academy. I'll give a nice little speech. I'll be proud to take their plaque. But I want you to tell this story. So it will never happen again."

Jones Academy is now the pride of the Choctaw Nation of Oklahoma, a premier Indian residency center for students attending schools in nearby Hartshorne, Oklahoma. Plans are for a small schedule of classes to begin again at Jones Academy in the fall of 2003. During the time of Tony Byars' stay, the school was under the jurisdiction of the federal government. There are as many perceptions and opinions about the Indian boarding school experience as there were students in attendance. Tony Byars, I know, would be proud to see his old school today—proud to see what Jones Academy has become under Choctaw management.

ARCHIE'S WAR

▼ ▼ ▼ ▼ ▼ ▼ ▼ ▼ ▼ ▼ ▼ ▼ ▼ ▼

North Carolina, 1969

Everybody's always interested in the Indian Wars. So I would like to tell you about a war that means a lot to me personally. It was the twenty-year war between myself and my Choctaw father. On many things we disagreed.

The war really began when another war was going on in Viet Nam. I felt we shouldn't be fighting it. My father was a World War II veteran, so he felt differently. I wore my hair well down my back. He wore his in a crew cut. I felt I was grown-up. He thought I was a child. On many things we disagreed.

My brother Danny was just two years older than me and when he volunteered to fight in Viet Nam, the whole family gathered at Houston Hobby Airport to see him off. My mother had arranged for a photographer to be there. She kept saying, "It might be the last picture of all of us together." The photographer had taken half-a-dozen shots and was about to leave when my father stopped him. "Just one more. I want at least one picture without him in it," he said, pointing to me. So I stepped aside.

When the plane had taken off and we were on our way to the parking lot, I said to my father, "You know it's a shame HE has to be going. It's more your war than it is his."

My father just stopped and looked at me. I walked away.

A year later, my father wrote and asked me to work with him on the pipeline for the summer. I was paying my way through college and needed the money, so I flew out to North Carolina to join him. But I got a haircut first, a shoulder-length haircut, at least.

As we were driving to his trailer house, my father said, "You're gonna have to cut some more of that hair off before you go to work."

"I already got a haircut."

"I know, just appease your old man," he said.

So the next morning I slept till ten, then drove into one of the nearby towns looking for a barbershop. I circled the courthouse square a few times till I spotted that candy cane pole you used to see outside a barbershop. When I entered the shop, there was nobody else there and the barber just looked at me.

"Look," I said, "my dad's making me get a haircut. Just do a little trimming, I'll pay you full price and be on my way."

"All right, I'll take care of you," he said, and I sat down in the barber chair. He started off with the scissors, clipping round the edges. Then I heard a sound that should've warned me. Uhuhhhhhhh. It was only the clippers, but it went on for far too long. And every time I tried to look down to the floor, to see the little pile of hair there, he'd slap my chin. "Look up, boy. I can't cut less you keep still."

Shortly, another customer opened the door and I felt a whoosh of a breeze on the back of my neck where I hadn't felt a breeze in years. "That'll do it," the barber said. He powdered me up and spun me around in the chair. "What do ya think?"

I was bald as a cue ball. "I don't think it's what I asked for. But I guess we can't do anything about it now." I reached for my wallet and he said, "Oh, that won't be necessary. Your father already took care of that."

DING! Round One went to Archie.

The next day began a stretch of six weeks in a row without a single day off, working with my father on the pipeline. Most of that time was actually spent under the pipeline, for that's how the welding was done. We'd climb into a ditch dug under the 42-inch diameter pipe. My father wore a helmet with a protective glass shield to look through, for he'd spend much of his day staring at a burning electrical arc as he'd draw a bead on that weld, tying the pipe together with a good clean weld.

Ever so often, he would hold out a gloved hand, without even looking at me, and I'd slap a welding rod into it. He'd attach it and go right back to that arc.

It was summertime, like I said, and it was hot. Well over 100 degrees, even hotter than that at the bottom of that hole, and we wore undershirts and three layers of khaki shirts to protect us from the falling sparks. I knew now why my dad always had blisters on his neck—from where a piece of falling trash metal would get under the collar. But when that happened, he couldn't flinch. He might have a piece of metal burning through his skin, but he had to stay right with that arc, to draw a good clean bead.

There were some characters on that pipeline. During a lunch break, I got to see old man Fiddler go through his favorite routine. He was nearing 65 years, but he was union so they kept him on. He'd follow the pipeline, picking up trash and used welding rods. And he'd say, "I get up every morning, look in the mirror, see my belly hanging out. I lean forward, tuck my shirt in, then look behind me, see

Archie and his squirrels at the old Tingle place, Pasadena, Texas

somethin' showin' back there. So I lean back, tuck it in good, but lawd, my belly be poppin' out, so I go to tuckin' it in again. Seem like I spend all my days tuckin' and aleanin', tuckin' and aleanin'. Life's hard when you're old."

We young ones, we would laugh at old Fiddler. I saw him do this dozens of times. And I would give anything to see him do it again.

And there was Jim, Big Jim, everybody called him. He was part German, had silvery hair and steely-blue eyes and he worked alone, up ahead of everybody else. It was his job to guide the pipe right over the hole. With a crane hoisting the pipe up, he'd push and position it right where it needed to be 'fore the crane would lower it down.

He seemed friendly enough, but if I tried to walk over to talk to him early in the morning, my father would say, "Get away from there! Don't touch that crane. Get on away."

Jim'd just shrug his shoulders and wave. I thought, "Why is my old man so mean?" That's what I thought.

One morning, about 11 o'clock, the foreman came walking up slow, then he leaned down into the trench.

"Archie," he called.

"What's wrong?" my dad asked, taking his helmet off.

"We're taking the rest of the day off. The crane hit a high voltage 'lectrical wire. Big Jim had his hand on the crane. He died."

"Ok," my dad said. "All right. See you tomorrow morning."

"Yeah," the foreman said, and he walked on to tell the next welder.

As that long, hot summer drew to a close, word went round about a storm, a hurricane blowing up on the coast. We caught the first heavy rainstorm one late afternoon, and my dad's truck got stuck. He was mad about somebody having to come help him, pull him out. When the truck backed up to his, he told me, "Get out and hook the tow chain up." I stepped out of the truck. By now the tires were spinning and his bumper was deep in the muddy soup.

He leaned out the window. "Do it, son, hook it up."

I looked at all the mud, and instead of hooking it to the axle, I just hooked the chain around the bumper; so when the tow truck started pulling, the bumper bent and the chain went flying. My dad was so mad. "You ain't got the sense God gave a man to get in out of the rain," he said to me. Then he climbed into the mud and hooked the chain around the axle himself. I just stood there looking at him.

When the tow truck started up, my father yelled, "Get out of the way, boy. Chain might pop. Move away." I just stood there, didn't move a muscle.

Finally, when he was pulled free, I undid the chain and climbed into the cab. My dad was hollering mad now. "Son, if that chain broke, it could cut your head off!"

I didn't reply till we were underway, then muttered to the window in a voice barely audible, "That would make you real happy. Then I'd be out of the picture completely. That would make your day." That's what I said to him. Now I'm not proud of everything I said, I'm just recounting the story.

We didn't speak maybe ten words for several days, till this job was over and the real storm blew in on the final day.

It started out a light rain and we smelled the pinewoods and it was sweet and clean, but when the rain fell heavy, the smell of diesel fuel stuck to your skin. With the storm coming, an old school bus came to pick the helpers up. I watched the bus roll by and waved at old man Fiddler. Then a face appeared and disappeared at the back of the bus. Looked to me like Big Jim. But he didn't wave. He just placed his ten fingers on the rear window and gazed at me with those steely-blue eyes, then vanished in the mist and the rain.

The wind was really blowing now; branches were flying off the trees. A bunch of workers piled into Dad's truck. There wasn't room for me.

"You're gonna have to ride on back," Dad said. "And son, I can't stop, once we get moving."

"Okay."

"No, listen to me. We're driving into a storm. We drive five miles an hour, we move as a group, so we don't pile up out here. If you fall off, roll out of the way and get on the first truck you can. Ain't nobody gonna stop for you. You hear me?"

"Yes sir." He turned away and started that clattering old diesel engine. I hoisted myself up and wrapped my left arm around the iron brace holding the welding rig to the back of the truck. Soon the smell of dust became the smell of mud, red clay mud slick with rainwater. When the storm hit, the rain broke the surface of the road like the tiny beaks of blind little birds, opening and closing. Then the rain hit like fat cold stones. And I was alone and I was cold and I felt like an abandoned child.

The first sheet of rain soaked through my every stitch of clothing: boots, socks, three shirts, jeans. When the wind hit, it came from the opposite direction as the rain, from behind me, and even though the cab broke the gale, it hit me with such force I watched three buttons pop off my khaki shirt.

A short while later, my arm cramped up and the sharp edge of the iron brace rubbed and blistered through the skin of my upper arm. I thought of moving, then saw the danger of falling off. A bump in the road, a gust of wind. So instead, I took to biting my tongue, then the inside of my cheek. Soft at first, then hard, hoping to focus on the lesser pain—and not the one in my arm. The harder I bit, the easier this became, until I tasted blood and ran my tongue across a deep swollen cut on the inside of my mouth.

I realized I had been shivering and crying for probably an hour.

And on we crawled. Twenty-six miles. Five miles per hour. In the cold and never-ending rain. When the truck finally pulled onto the makeshift parking lot, my father unwrapped my arm from the welding brace and lifted me onto the ground. I was shivering and sobbing and my teeth were chattering hard.

"What were you thinking?" he asked me.

"I was scared. I thought I might die."

"What did you do?"

"I hung on. And I prayed."

He just nodded; then he reached up and grabbed short bristles of my hair, down to my scalp, and gave it a good hard tug.

"You are all right," he said. And at that moment, I knew that I was. I watched my father's tan khakis turn dark brown in the downpour.

"Ain't got the sense God gave a man to get in out of the rain," I told him. He closed his eyes and when he re-opened them, it was just he and I, just the two of us. The other trucks were pulling away. There we stood in the pouring down rain.

I would like to tell you that our lives changed from that moment on, but life doesn't work that way. Our wars went on for several years, until I had my own son, Jacob, and began to see fatherhood from the other side.

The last ten years of his life my father became my finest, deepest friend. But I think he always knew he would be. From that long, hot summer on the pipeline, we knew that when darkness falls at noon, when the rain turns to cold hard stones, we knew we prayed to the same God. We clung to the same thin thread of His mercy. This my father gave to me. And this I gave to my son.

SALTYPIE

▼ ▼ ▼ ▼ ▼ ▼ ▼ ▼ ▼ ▼ ▼ ▼ ▼ ▼ ▼ ▼

*A Family Allegory of a Journey from
Darkness into Light*

*My father, Archie Daniel Tingle, Junior, was born in Indian
Territory, Oklahoma. When he was still a toddler the family moved
to Pasadena, Texas.*

My grandparents lived in a white frame house I still see clearly in my mind, for it was in that house I received the worst whopping I ever got in my entire life.

My Aunt Bobbie did the honors on my backside. I had dragged a dining room chair into the living room and scooted it real close to the television set, just like I had seen my grandmother do. I watched television for about an hour, then decided I needed a drink of water. I dashed to the kitchen at the back of the house. Grandmother—Mawmaw, I called her—always kept a big jar of cold water in the refrigerator. I made sure nobody was watching and drank several deep gulps straight from the jar, then wiped my lips on my sleeve, just like my dad always did.

I had just shut the door to the refrigerator—we always

called it an ice-box—when I heard a scraping sound, then a loud crash, coming from the living room. It was my grandmother, stumbling over my chair.

Along came my Aunt Bobbie. She was big and strong and everybody said you didn't want Aunt Bobbie mad at you. She scooped me up by the arm, the tender part by the armpit, and hurried me out to the back porch, where she proceeded to whip me good!

"Don't you ever move furniture from one place to another without putting it right back where you got it!" she said between swings. "Not in this house!"

She finally turned loose of me and I stood there crying, too afraid to leave, too afraid to even say, "Yes, ma'am." I just stood there sniffling and sobbing. I thought about wiping my runny nose on my sleeve, then decided I better not as long as she was there. My dad always wiped his nose that way, but I figured he probably wouldn't if he'd just got a whipping from Aunt Bobbie.

As soon as she was gone, I ran to a wooden bench in the grape arbor. I sat there for a little while till Mawmaw came out and sat beside me.

"Whooping'll go away, boy," she said. "Whooping goes away." I didn't think it would ever go away—it stung bad!

"That was some kind of saltypie from your Aunt Bobbie," Mawmaw said. "That was sure enough some kind of saltypie."

There always seemed to be a quiet laugh on the other side of my grandmother's words. The sting didn't exactly go away, but with my grandmother there, it was sort of like dipping my bottom in warm bathwater. It felt better.

We sat together for a long time. That was Mawmaw's way. Then she stood up and in that shuffling way she had of walking, she moved towards the chicken house, calling over her shoulder, "Chickens need afeedin'." She knew I would follow right along behind her, for feeding the chickens and gathering eggs was one of my favorite things to do. She had taught me how to scootch those hens out of the way and move your hand real quick before your hand got pecked.

We filled a tin bucket with eggs and carried them to a dark room in back of the garage, where my grandfather had built a light board. It had once been a porcelain table with wooden legs. Pawpaw had removed the porcelain top and replaced it with a glass pane with light bulbs under it. A black electrical cord ran from the table to the wall socket, snaking across the dirt and sawdust floor. When the switch was flipped, the room filled with shafts of yellow light lifting from the table to the ceiling.

We had to see if any of the eggs were fertilized, meaning they wouldn't be any good to eat. Fertilized eggs had little flecks of blood and you didn't want that showing up in your fried eggs. Mawmaw would place the eggs on the table, one at a time, and I would roll them over, looking closely for any sign of a red spot.

"Look real good," she'd say, "and don't you trick me!"

"I won't trick you, Mawmaw."

If I saw a fertilized egg, and there were plenty, I'd say, probably way too loud, knowing how I was, "There's one, Mawmaw!"

"Where?"

"Right here it is!" She would take the egg and move it real close to her eyes, like she was verifying, then she'd throw it in a 50-gallon oil drum she used for a trash can. The egg would smash into white pieces of eggshell and yellow and red insides and ooze down the side of the oil drum.

Mawmaw would laugh that quiet funny laugh, like

there was so much more to laugh at than you would ever know. "That's some kind of saltypie for those chicken eggs, boy," she would say. "Some kind of saltypie."

My grandmother was a strong woman, a special woman, even I knew that. My big brother might get away with calling me "Ignurnt!" at home, but when I was with my grandmother, I felt safe. Our family, the Tingle family, it was her family. Those five boys and two girls, my dad and his brothers and sisters, they were her children, there was no doubt about that.

I used to imagine what it was like for her, that first day in Pasadena, that first day in her new home, after the long trip from Oklahoma. There she was, parting the white lace curtains on the front window and catching her first glimpse of early morning comings and goings in her new neighborhood. She timidly eased the door open and stepped out on the front porch to greet the dawn.

She never saw the boy that threw the stone that cut her face. It sent her stumbling and reeling inside, slamming the door behind her. That white cotton dress she wore slid against the surface of the pine door and she crumpled in a heap on the floor, sobbing. My father was two at the time; he ran to see what all the commotion was. There he saw his mother sitting on the living room floor, her hands covering her face. It looked like the peep-eye game to him.

He crawled into her lap and saw shiny red juice squishing from between her fingertips. It looked to him like sweet and sour cherry pie filling bubbling up from the criss-cross crust of Mawmaw's pies. He reached his finger to her face to get a taste of it, then touched his fingertip to his lips.

"Saltypie!" he said, spitting as he said it. "Saltypie!"

Mawmaw pulled her hands apart and looked down at him. She was crying and bleeding everywhere, on her dress, all over her face and neck. She saw the ugly face he was making, his lips red with her blood.

"Saltypie," she said. "That is sure enough some kind of saltypie." She held him close to her chest and went to laughing and crying, rocking back and forth and all the time saying, "Sure enough, that was some kind of saltypie, with those rocks. Some kind of saltypie, boy. Sure was."

She was still laughing about it at the supper table that night, when she told my Pawpaw why she had a bandage across her cheek. She had to grab his arm and plead with him not to go out into the neighborhood, 'cause he wanted to find out who it was and go whip somebody's daddy, but it wouldn't have done any good—she never saw the boy that threw the stone that cut her face.

I really loved my grandmother, but I didn't give her the respect she deserved, not really, till I was eight years old. I had talked my Pawpaw into letting me have my very own cup of coffee to saucer and blow like he did. We sat at a circle of a table in the kitchen, seven grown-ups and a few children crowded around. I sat right next to Pawpaw, ready to have my first cup of coffee at breakfast. Here came Mawmaw filling up the cups.

She had what I thought was a disgusting habit. Mawmaw would put her thumb in the empty cup, just over the rim, and pour the coffee till it reached her first knuckle, then shake the hot coffee off, lick her thumb to cool it, and put it in the next cup. When she came to me, I put my hand over the cup and wouldn't let her put her thumb in.

As soon as I did that, everybody stopped talking. My Pawpaw was reaching for the butter, but instead of picking the butter dish up, he slowly moved his hand back to his lap and looked down at his plate. Nobody moved for what seemed like a long time. I slid my hand off my cup, but whatever I had done, I knew it was too late to take it back. I heard a chair scrape and looked up under my eyelids. It was Aunt Bobbie. She was looking right at me as she walked around the table and I could see she was rolling her sleeves up as she walked.

In my mind, it was Saturday morning and I was Roadrunner outrunning Coyote, laughing and blowing dust in his face. That daydream lasted for about three seconds. It was Saturday morning all right, but I wasn't outrunning anybody. I was frozen in blood-curdling terror.

Aunt Bobbie scooped me up and carried me to the screened-in back porch. I anticipated a whipping to end all whippings, one with the added disgrace of being the morning's entertainment for cousins and aunts and uncles who would joke about it for years. Aunt Bobbie positioned me in a corner, nodded to let me know which way to lean, then she squared her feet just the right distance from her target. She gripped my arm hard with her left hand and lifted her right hand. I made a scrunching face and squeezed my eyes tight shut.

Nothing happened. I opened my eyes and glanced over at her feet. She hadn't moved an inch, so I made the face and squeezed my eyes shut again. Still nothing. I felt her loosen her grip on my arm, so I sneaked a peak at her raised hand, the striking one. It was still poised, right in the middle of mid-whoop. I wasn't out of this one yet.

"You don't know, do you, boy?" she said.

"No, ma'am, I don't know. If they try to tell me, I won't listen, I promise. I don't want to know."

Aunt Bobbie laughed and looked me over like she was seeing me for the first time. She let go of my arm and I stood up real slow.

"Bless your heart," she said. "All these years and you

Mawmaw and grandchild on the front porch at the old house

don't know. Your grandmother is blind, boy. That's why you have to help her with the eggs. That's why you get in trouble for moving the furniture around. That's why she uses her thumb when she's pouring coffee, so she'll know when the cup is full. Mercy, boy, you didn't know."

She swatted at me playful-like and I jumped like I'd been shot.

"I'm not gonna hurt you, son," Aunt Bobbie said, laughing and smiling and shaking her head. "Just go on back there and let your grandmother do what she has to do."

I couldn't believe it. I was eight years old and I didn't realize my grandmother was blind. That night at the evening talking time, when everybody sat under the trees in outdoor chairs and on the back porch steps and drank their favorite beverage, I asked my uncle how come Mawmaw was blind.

"Cataracts," he said, "that's what the doctors say. Cataracts. But some people say her eyes have never been exactly right since she got hit with those rocks. That was some kind of saltypie, with them boys throwing rocks at your grandmother."

"Who was it? Do we know 'em?" I asked.

"No, I don't reckon we'll ever know who did that. Some things are just too cowardly to even brag about."

He sat without talking for a long time. We listened to the sounds of the chickens roosting and the distant whisper of cars driving by on the asphalt road. I smelled the blooming gardenias that Mawmaw kept tucked real close to the house.

"Why did they do it?"

"Your grandmother was Indian. That was enough back then," my uncle said. A mosquito buzzed around my ear. I went to slap it but a little breeze blew up, carrying the mosquito off to draw somebody else's blood and washing the backyard with the soft music of rustling corn stalks. At our house the mosquitoes would eat you alive outside at night, but they never were that bad at Mawmaw's.

It always seemed if you waited long enough and quiet enough at Mawmaw's house, you would know things that ought to be known. If you got in a hurry, you'd go away and leave those things behind and maybe never know 'em. I was always glad when I could stay awake long enough to listen to those secret sounds you only heard at Mawmaw's.

Aunt Bobbie brought me a blanket and wrapped it tight around me. "What is saltypie?" I asked her. She stooped over and touched my hair.

"It's a way of dealing with trouble, son. Sometimes you don't know where the trouble comes from. You just kinda shrug it off, say 'saltypie.' It helps you carry on."

I fell asleep that night and didn't wake up till my dad was carrying me to the car for the hour trip home.

The years passed by taking forever. We went to Mawmaw's less often, then almost not at all. Sometimes it seemed the only thing that made any sense was the sweet feel of my leather basketball. Whatever happened at home, I could always go outside and dribble and dribble, thump, thump, thumping all through junior high and high school. I could make seven of ten free throws with my eyes closed. It was my game, all I knew or would ever need to know.

Then somewhere in the midst of all this dribbling and jumping, I realized that if I wanted a home anything like Mawmaw's, I would have to make it myself.

I was a junior at the University of Texas in Austin when I got the call we all know is coming some day.

"Your grandmother is in Ben Taub Hospital, downtown Houston, fourth floor. Come right away." The note was tacked to my door when I got home from classes.

In ten minutes, I was on the road. I drove the four hours to Houston and found the parking lot to Ben Taub Hospital, near Hermann Park Zoo. I dashed inside and took the elevator to the fourth floor waiting room. It was filled with people, cramped together and sitting and standing everywhere. I looked around for a familiar face. Then it dawned on me—they were all familiar faces. The whole Tingle clan was gathered together.

They told me my grandmother was undergoing one of the first eye transplant surgeries in the city of Houston. We were all there to support her. I found a corner and settled down to listen. Most of the stories floating around were about my grandmother.

Relatives who hadn't seen each other in a few years caught everybody up on what they'd been doing. I heard somebody say we may be waiting for days before the doctors would know anything.

We did wait for days, four days, going through the entire gamut of family emotions. We laughed, teased, fought, then laughed all over again to see that nobody had really changed, just grown fatter, skinnier, and balder. Some folks took shifts with other family members, a husband going to work, a wife leaving for a half-day to feed the dog and do errands, but by the evening of the fourth day, we were all there waiting for news.

About an hour before sundown, the doctor stuck his head through the door and said, "We'll know soon." A quiet but remarkable shift occurred in the room. The light streaming through the window took on a copper color, bouncing and reflecting off downtown skyscrapers till it floated above the green waiting-room carpet. It reminded me of the late afternoon sun filtering through the live oaks and settling on the thick Saint Augustine grass in Mawmaw's backyard.

The spirit of who we were as a family, as a people, was coming alive in the room. It was palpable and alive—as alive as the unseen cicadas that hummed their night music in the Choctaw river bottoms from whence we had come. The stories continued, but there were fewer words now and much silent nodding. Many heads were bowed to the moment. In the common gesture of long-remembered ritual, the youngest to the oldest began to speak.

Aunt Mary told of Mawmaw making her go to school when she played sick.

"She always knew!" she said, and everybody laughed.

Somebody else talked about her homemade ice cream and how they used to sit on the freezer while one of the older boys cranked. Somebody told about how hard it had been for Mawmaw at boarding school—Wheelock Academy in Oklahoma—especially after her father died and there was nobody to take her home for Christmas.

I told about helping Mawmaw feed the chickens.

We listened like we were all sharing the same sweet dream for over an hour, till everybody had spoken except my father. He stood up and took his welding cap off, twisting it in his hands in front of him. He was shy and he kept us waiting for a long time. The doctor looked through the small windowpane on the door and motioned to my father. They spoke in the hallway and my father returned.

I have never been so proud of him as I was that day. It was so right that my father, who had given us this word 50 years ago in a moment of childhood misunderstanding, would take it away in a moment of enlightenment. He lifted his eyes and spoke.

"No more saltypie," he said. "Mawmaw can see."

It seemed like everything my family had gone through had led up to this moment.

"No more saltypie. Your grandmother can see."

$\mathcal{W}$E ARE A PEOPLE OF MIRACLES

▼ ▼ ▼ ▼ ▼ ▼ ▼ ▼ ▼ ▼ ▼ ▼ ▼ ▼ ▼ ▼ ▼

Someone always talked about how we came to be in America. But our ancestors tell us that the Lord kneaded us out of this place. We didn't come from faraway places. We didn't come from faraway lands. We were kneaded out of this place. And we are never to sell the land. The Great Spirit will teach us how not to sell. And one day when he comes back, he will know his people.

That is what Estelline Tubby said. "We were kneaded out of this place."

We are clay people.
We are a people of miracles.

We have survived the walking; it is behind us.
We have survived the blankets; they are the tattered cloth of the past.

The dark dirt of Mississippi
The waters of Misha Sopokni
The red clay of Okla Homma

Chief Gregory Pyle and Assistant Chief Mike Bailey lead hundreds of Choctaws on a Trail of Tears Memorial Walk

They mingle with our bones.
We are clay people.
We are a people of miracles.

We are not vanishing; we are not going anywhere.
We live here.
We live in Louisiana, Alabama, Mississippi, Texas,
    Oklahoma.
We live in California.
We live in Washington, D.C.
We are everywhere.

We have been scattered like seeds upon the wind,
But like the good seed that we are,
We found the earth,

We found the water
And we grew…
For like a tree with many branches,
We are nourished by our roots.

We are clay people.
We are a people of miracles.

We are people of this land.
We are Americans.
And from the War of 1812,
We fought alongside Red, White, and Blue.
We are the Codetalkers of World War One.
We love our frybread and our stickball and our
    baseball, too.

The old Choctaw Capitol, Tushka Homma, Oklahoma

We are Americans,
And like all Americans,
We love our freedom.

We love the red brick of our capitol,
The gentle slope of our hillsides,
The fat bellies of our babies,
The green of our graveyards.
We love to sit beside the cool waters of our rivers.
We are a good people.
We are Okla Achukma.
We are a great people.
We are the Choctaw Nation.

We are clay people.
We are a people of miracles.

GLOSSARY OF CHOCTAW WORDS

aba, vba: heaven; divine

achufa, achafa: one

achukma: good

ala: one who arrives or comes

alla: child; children

ant: come and…

ant ia: go past here

bok: river

cha: and

chihot, chia hat: art thou

Chissus, Chisas: Jesus

chisno: thou; thine

chitto, chito: big; heavy

falamat: return; bring back

feyna, fehna: much; very

ha: it

hatak: man

hina: road; pathway

hoke: okay, a way of saying, "yes"

holitopa: spirit; dear; valuable

hoyo: look for; search

ia: to go

ilbasha: miserable; poor-in-spirit; humble

ish: you (singular)

isht: with

isht-ayo: to be sorted with

lashke: I shall; let me

li: I

ma: an exclamation often heard in personal salutations, for which there is no corresponding word in English

minti: to come; to start this way

miniti; mihinti: he is coming

misha: beyond; further

nitak: day

nowa: to walk; traveler

okchako: bright blue

okla: people; tribe; nation

ona: to go to; to reach

pi: us; we

pikmano: the time when we

pulla: necessary; certainly

shilombish: spirit

sapokni: my grandmother

sipokni: old; ancient

tuklo: two

tuchina: three

umala: on arrival

ut: subject marker, as in *a* or *the*

yali: I weep

yukpa: to laugh; joy

A comment on Choctaw-English translation

Choctaw hymns pose difficulties for literal English translation. Some Choctaw hymns and religious songs rely on vocables, as do the religious ceremonial songs of many other tribes. These vocables have deeply traditional meanings and values, for which corresponding words may not exist in English. Further, some hymns of Christian-European origin have been translated into Choctaw so that their essential spiritual meaning is maintained, although the words themselves may be quite different when a literal translation is attempted.

Choctaw Hymns

Amazing Grace

Shilombish Holitopa ma!
Ish minti pulla cha,
Hatak ilbusha pia ha
Ish pi yukpalashke.

Literal English translation:
My Holy Spirit!
Thou must come,
We are suffering men
Bring us joy.

On Jordan's Stormy Banks
by Samuel Stennett
(chorus)
We are bound for the Promised
Land,
We are bound for the Promised
Land!
O, who will come and go with me?
We are bound for the Promised
Land.

Nitak ishtaiyopikmuno,
Chisus ut mihintit,
Um ulla holitopa ma!
Chi hot aya lishke.

Literal English translation:
Finally, on the last day,
Jesus is coming,
O holy child!
I am going with thee.

FURTHER READINGS ON THE CHOCTAWS

JUVENILE TITLES

Frye, Mary. *The Pashofa Pole.* Durant: Choctaw Nation of Oklahoma, 2000.
McKee, Jesse. *The Choctaws.* New York: Chelsea House Publishers, 1989.

FICTION FOR ADULTS

Owens, Louis. *The Sharpest Sight.* Norman: University of Oklahoma Press, 1992.
Askew, Rilla. *The Mercy Seat.* New York: Viking Penguin, 1997.

NON-FICTION FOR ADULTS

Debo, Angie. *The Rise And Fall of The Choctaw Republic.* Norman: University of Oklahoma Press, 1934.
DeRosier, Arthur. *The Removal of The Choctaw Indians.* Knoxville: The University of Tennessee Press, 1970.
Haag, Marcia and Henry Willis. *Choctaw Language And Culture.* Norman: University of Oklahoma Press, 2001.

POETRY

Barnes, Jim. *On Native Ground.* Norman: University of Oklahoma Press, 1997.